The Man Who Stole Tomorrow

C.O. Shepherdson

Book Title: *The Man Who Stole Tomorrow*
Written by: C.O. Shepherdson
Illustrated by: Learning Engineered Publishing®
Published by: Learning Engineered Publishing®, Tallahassee, Florida https://LearningEngineeredPublishing.com

Library of Congress Control Number: 2026931[illegible]5
ISBN (Paperback): 978-1-965741-66-5

First Edition: 2026

Printed & Created in: United States of America

Learning Engineered Publishing® (U.S. Reg. No. 3,057,038) is a division of Learning Engineered, LLC, and a subsidiary of Carpe Diem Unlimited Holdings, Inc.

Contents

Epigraph VI

Dedication VII

A Note to the Reader VIII

Author's Note IX

Content Warning XIV

1. Chapter 1 1
2. Chapter 2 6
3. Chapter 3 10
4. Chapter 4 14
5. Chapter 5 17
6. Chapter 6 20
7. Chapter 7 23
8. Chapter 8 27
9. Chapter 9 30
10. Chapter 10 34
11. Chapter 11 37

12. Chapter 12 40
13. Chapter 13 43
14. Chapter 14 45
15. Chapter 15 47
16. Chapter 16 51
17. Chapter 17 55
18. Chapter 18 58
19. Chapter 19 62
20. Chapter 20 64
21. Chapter 21 67
22. Chapter 22 69
23. Chapter 23 74
24. Chapter 24 76
25. Chapter 25 78
26. Chapter 26 81
27. Chapter 27 83
28. Chapter 28 86
29. Chapter 29 89
30. Chapter 30 93
31. Chapter 31 96
32. Chapter 32 99
33. Chapter 33 102

Epilogue 106
Night Light 107
The Widening Witness 108

Epigraph

And Jesus said unto him,
Verily I say unto thee,
To day shalt thou be with me in paradise.
—Luke 23:43 (KJV)

Dedication

To Elise, Theo, and Lydia Grace—

and every grandchild whose tomorrow I hope to meet—
This story begins on the morning my daughter becomes a woman
and ends the days after Easter.

I wrote it because every father carries two lives inside him—
the one he lived,
and the one he still hopes his children will never have to survive.

Read it.
Burn it.
Set it free.

All I ask is that whatever good this book ever does
belongs to my wife and children
as long as words endure.

I am still becoming the man I should have been.
I love you more than you will ever know.

—Dad/ Micah Christian Shepherdson

A Note to the Reader

This story is not written to persuade, instruct, or debate.

It is written to tell the truth as faithfully as fiction allows.

Move slowly.

Pause when needed.

Let silence do some of the work.

Nothing in these pages asks you to agree.

Only to bear witness.

Author's Note

This book began as a dream.

Not a single dream, but thirty-three separate dreams spread across twelve years—

night-dreams, day-dreams, fragments that arrived out of order, unconnected, insistent.

Memories that returned with new color,

and stories shared with me over the years by family, friends,

and people whose lives brushed mine at the right moment.

For years I carried them without understanding the shape.

Then came a final dream that revealed the arc—

borrowed days,

a countdown from Lydia Grace's eighteenth birthday

to the third day after death.

Only then could I place the fragments in order

and see the story whole.

I also carry my own near-death experience—

something I rarely speak about,

something that marked me without explaining itself.

I do not treat it as doctrine,

but it opened a window in me

to the way a soul tries to make sense of mercy, regret, forgiveness,

and the quiet ways God enters a life.

Dates and days in this story

do not belong to any single calendar.

They appeared as they came to me in dreams—

fractured,

symbolic,

untethered.

Read them not as chronology,

but as the rhythm of a soul learning to tell time again.

They move in kairos, not chronos—

in the kind of time where grace arrives early,

and resurrection does not wait for the calendar to agree with it.

I grew up in a quiet home church—

no stages,

no spotlights,

just the Kingdom of God breaking in

around an ordinary table.

After my father died,

I was swept into louder currents,

chasing the next great move of God.

For years I rode that whirlwind.

Eventually I stepped away—

not from the body of Christ,

but from the noise—

to unlearn and remember what I had first known as a boy:

the gospel lived out in the daily rhythm of family and neighbors,

in the still, small voice.

The story you are about to read is fiction—

a mythic meditation on sin, confession,

and what resurrection might feel like

inside a man who finally stopped running from grace.

This story was dreamed in that quieter place.

The resurrections here are not dramatic revivals.

They are breakfast.

They are children passing butter.

They are the Kingdom coming without observation—

exactly as I have come to know it again.

Nothing here is offered as a map of the unseen world—

of heaven, judgment, or resurrection as fixed geography.

These are images given in the grammar of dream,

where a soul's reckoning can be rendered as weather, fire, bread, nails, and names.

They do not claim to explain what lies beyond,

only what grace can do within:

bringing buried truth into the light,

and teaching a man—slowly, painfully—

how to live without hiding.

If the scenes feel strange at times,

let them remain strange.

They were not written to prove anything,

but to bear witness.

If some part of this helps you imagine grace more clearly,

or forgiveness more honestly,

or resurrection more quietly,

then the dream has done its work.

I once imagined this book would only be read when I was gone.

I release it now

because true confession belongs to the living.

—C.O. Shepherdson

Content Warning

This novel engages deeply with abortion, regret, hidden sin, spiritual reckoning, and the long work of repentance.

It contains visionary and symbolic encounters involving unborn children, grief, and moral responsibility.

These moments are written as dream-language rather than literal description,
but they may be emotionally intense for some readers.

This book is not written to shock, persuade, or argue,
but to explore how grace enters the places we most avoid naming.

If you carry wounds in this area,
please read gently.

If you carry guilt,
don't rush.

If you carry grief,
you are not alone in these pages.

Chapter 1

The morning Lydia Grace turned eighteen, I woke up already dead.

I knew it before my eyes opened.

The bedroom smelled like a tomb cracked open too soon: wet limestone, blood, and the faint sweetness of magnolia blossoms rotting on the vine.

Elise was still asleep beside me, breathing soft and steady the way she has every night since December 1, 2013—the day she married a man who still had blood on his hands he hadn't confessed yet.

Twenty-three years, three months, and twenty days of borrowed tomorrows.

I slipped out of bed without waking her, joints popping like dry kindling, and walked barefoot through the house that still carried crayon ghosts on the baseboards and the echo of little-girl laughter in the hallway.

Outside, the Louisiana dawn was the color of a bruise.

I stepped onto the back porch and saw it.

My obituary nailed to the pecan tree we planted the day Lydia Grace was born.

A sheet of yellow legal paper, edges curled from the night's dew, pierced clean through with a sixteen-penny nail. The same kind I used to build her treehouse when she was six. The one she outgrew at twelve and I never finished.

I knew the handwriting before I crossed the yard.

All caps.

Angry.

Nineteen-year-old me trying to look fearless.

MICAH CHRISTIAN Shepherdson

Husband of Elise (23 years, 3 months, 20 days)

Father of Lydia Grace and Theo, murderer of Mercy Joy

Died today

Age 67

Cause of death: too many mercies refused.

Services: none.

Tell Lydia Grace I finally became her father.

I reached up and touched the paper.

It was warm. Fever-warm.

I tried to pull the nail free. It wouldn't come. The wood had already grown around it like it had been there for decades.

That's when I heard the horse.

Slow, deliberate hooves on gravel. Not a sound you hear in this neighborhood anymore.

I turned.

He stood at the end of the driveway wearing my father's face the day Daddy died. Same gray Stetson pulled low. Same hollow eyes that had already seen the end and decided not to warn anybody.

The rider swung down without a sound and took three steps toward me. The temperature dropped so fast the dew on the grass crackled into frost.

"Morning, son," he said, and it was Daddy's voice exactly, except it came from somewhere behind the teeth.

My mouth went dry.

"You're not him."

He smiled the way Daddy smiled the day he caught me lying about where I'd been.

"I'm what comes when a man keeps borrowing tomorrows he was never meant to have," he said.

He reached into the Carhartt coat we buried Daddy in and pulled out a single page torn from a book I recognized instantly.

Thick paper.

Gold edges.

Red letters.

My name was written in the margin in my own nineteen-year-old scrawl.

And someone had drawn a line through it in red so dark it looked wet.

He let the page fall.

It landed face-up in the frost.

The rider tipped his hat.

“You’ve got thirty-three days to put that name back where it belongs,” he said. “Starting with the birthday girl inside, and the wife who’s loved you through every lie.”

Then he mounted up and rode straight into the rising sun like the horizon had been waiting eighteen years to open its mouth and swallow him whole.

I stood there barefoot until the page in the grass began to smoke without flame.

The obituary was gone from the tree.

Only the nail remained, dripping something darker than rust.

Lydia Grace’s eighteenth birthday had just begun.

And I had exactly thirty-three days to become the husband Elise married

and the father Lydia Grace and Theo deserved.

I looked back at the house.

Through the kitchen window I could see her standing at the counter in her pajamas, eighteen years old today, pouring cereal like the world hadn’t just ended.

I whispered the only prayer I had.

“Lord, let me live long enough to die right.”

Then I walked inside, to tell my daughter happy birthday

and to start stealing back every tomorrow I threw away.

The first one began now.

Chapter 2

I never made it to the kitchen to say happy birthday.

I was two steps from the back door when the sunrise went dark.

Not clouds.

Not an eclipse.

The sun simply stopped, like someone hit pause on the sky.

The light turned the color of old blood and the air thickened until it felt like sorrow.

Elise's scream came from inside the house, high and sharp the way it was the night Lydia Grace was born.

I ran.

The back door slammed open against the wall and I saw her standing in the living room, one hand over her mouth, the other pointing at the far wall.

There was a woman there.

She stood between the couch and the television, barefoot on our ugly beige carpet, wearing a dress made of living fire that didn't burn anything it touched.

Her hair moved like it was underwater.

Her belly was round with the child I paid to erase in 1987.

She was fifty years old and nineteen at the same time.

Her eyes were galaxies.

I knew her before she spoke.

She was the daughter I murdered.

She opened her mouth and the voice that came out was every lullaby Elise ever sang to Lydia Grace, braided with the sound of a thousand mothers weeping in clinic parking lots.

"Name me," she said.

The words hit me like a fist in the sternum.

I dropped to my knees on the same spot where Lydia Grace took her first steps.

Elise was frozen, tears streaming, unable to move.

The woman took one step forward.

The carpet smoked where her feet touched but did not burn.

"You paid $187.33 to erase me," she said.

"That was the exact cost of the procedure plus tax."

She reached into the fire of her dress and pulled out a crumpled receipt, yellowed and stained.

She let it fall.

It landed on the coffee table next to Lydia Grace's birthday cake.

The total was still circled in red pen.

I tried to speak.

My throat was full of gravel and graves.

She knelt in front of me, fire brushing my face without heat and placed her hand on my chest.

"I forgave you the day you paid," she whispered.

She pressed harder.

I felt every heartbeat I stole from her.

Fifty years' worth in one second.

My ribs cracked open as the veil in the temple.

Light poured out of the wound, white and blinding.

Elise screamed again, but this time it sounded like worship.

The woman leaned close enough that I could smell the womb I never let her leave.

"Thirty-two days," she said.

"That's how long you have to make me your daughter again."

Then she stood, turned, and walked straight through the wall.

The sunrise came back.

The smoke-and-magnolia was gone.

Only the receipt remained on the table, burning without flame.

Elise finally found her voice.

"Who was that, Micah?"

I looked at the receipt.

The total was circled in fresh blood.

I picked it up with shaking hands.

On the back, in handwriting I didn't recognize, were five words:

Her name is Mercy Joy.

I folded the paper and put it in my pocket.

Thirty-two days left—time enough, perhaps, to give my murdered daughter the only thing she ever wanted from me.

A father.

And a name.

Tomorrow was already bleeding.

Chapter 3

I didn't sleep.

I sat in the dark living room with the receipt in my fist and Mercy Joy's name burning a hole through my palm.

Elise finally passed out on the couch around four, exhausted from questions I couldn't answer yet.

Lydia Grace locked herself in her room after the party that never happened—eighteen candles still unlit on a cake that smelled like smoke and accusation.

At 5:47 a.m. I heard the truck keys rattle on the hook by the door.

They moved by themselves.

I watched them lift, swing once, and drop into my lap like a child tossing me a gift.

I knew what came next.

I walked outside in yesterday's clothes, barefoot again, and climbed into the old Ford I hadn't driven since the stroke scare two years ago.

The engine turned over on the first try.

The gauge sat on E.

I pulled out of the driveway anyway.

The rearview mirror was cracked down the middle.

That's when I saw him.

A boy, maybe eight years old, sitting in the middle of the back seat like he'd been there the whole time.

Dark curls.

My nose.

Elise's mouth.

And eyes that had never blinked in this world.

He wore footie pajamas the color of the sky right before a tornado.

He smiled at me in the mirror and the crack between us disappeared.

"Hi, Daddy," he said.

The voice was wind chimes and graves opening.

I pulled over on the side of the road, gravel popping under the tires, and turned around.

He was still there.

Real enough to touch.

I reached back.

My hand passed through empty air and cold that felt like drowning.

He never stopped smiling.

"I waited a long time," he said.

"You kept picking other things."

I couldn't breathe.

He leaned forward, small hands on the back of my seat, and whispered like we were telling secrets at a sleepover nobody else was invited to.

"I'm the son you never let breathe.

But I'm breathing now."

Then he pointed out the windshield.

About fifty yards ahead, the road simply ended.

Not a dead-end sign.

The asphalt just stopped, like God had run out of ink.

Beyond it was nothing but white light and the sound of a heartbeat that wasn't mine.

The boy climbed into the front seat beside me, light as air.

He put his hand on my arm and suddenly I could feel every kick he never got to give Elise's belly.

"I forgive you too," he said.

"Thirty-one days.

Not much time at all."

He looked up at me with eyes older than time.

"Drive, Daddy.

There's someone you still need to bury

before you can carry me home."

Then he vanished.

The truck radio came on by itself.

It was playing the lullaby Elise sang to Lydia Grace when she was born.

Only the words had changed.

Instead of hush little baby, it was singing my name.

Micah Christian Shepherdson

Micah Christian Shepherdson

Don't you cry...

I put the truck in drive and rolled toward the place where the road ended and the light began.

The radio kept singing.

I didn't turn it off.

I deserved every note.

Chapter 4

I came home at noon with graveyard dirt still under my fingernails and the taste of rust in my mouth.

Elise was waiting in the kitchen, arms crossed, eyes red from crying or not crying—I couldn't tell anymore.

Lydia Grace's door was shut.

Theo's old Tonka trucks sat in a silent line on the windowsill like soldiers waiting for a war that never came.

I opened my mouth to tell her everything.

What came out was not my voice.

It was nineteen-year-old me, cocky and terrified, the night I came home late with some other girl's perfume on my shirt and a lie already rehearsed.

"Hey babe, nothin' happened. I swear. You know you're the only one."

Elise flinched like I'd struck her.

The words kept coming in that same teenage drawl, the one she hadn't heard in forty-five years.

"I was just hangin' out. You're overreacting."

I tried to stop.

My tongue wouldn't obey.

I watched her face move through grief she'd already lived once and buried.

"Stop it," she whispered.

I couldn't.

The boy kept talking, hands in pockets, shifting his weight like he was waiting to be grounded.

"I'm sorry, okay? Can we just drop it?"

I grabbed the counter to keep from falling.

Then the second voice came.

Lower.

Older.

The voice I use when I pray alone in the dark.

It spoke at the same time as the boy, like two radio stations bleeding into each other.

"I paid for an abortion with the money I was saving for your ring.

I never told you.

I've carried her every day we've been married."

Swagger and confession fought inside my mouth until blood ran from my nose.

Elise heard both.

She heard the boy who betrayed her before she ever said yes.

She heard the man who wore her ring for twenty-three years, three months, and twenty-three days while hiding a grave.

She backed away until her shoulders touched the refrigerator.

The voices stopped.

Silence rushed in.

I dropped to my knees on the same spot where I once proposed with a ring pop because I couldn't afford real gold yet.

Understood.

Same rules. Same restraint. Same breath.

Chapter 5

I preached my last sermon to the room I built on lies.

The sanctuary was empty except for dust and the echo of words I no longer trusted myself to say.

The pulpit still smelled like lemon oil and old ambition.

I stood where I had stood for twenty-three years and realized I could no longer remember which sentences had been true and which ones I had borrowed to survive.

I opened my mouth.

Nothing came out.

Not doubt.

Not faith.

Just silence.

The kind that arrives when a voice finally refuses to perform.

I stepped down from the platform.

The floorboards creaked like they were relieved.

Behind the pulpit, the wall where the cross once hung was bare.

Only the outline remained—lighter than the surrounding paint, like a scar that remembered its own healing.

I touched it.

The wood was warm.

I heard Asher's voice—not aloud, but inside the place where lies used to live.

"Say it, Daddy."

I swallowed.

"I don't know how to be clean," I said.

The room didn't answer.

Instead, the doors at the back of the sanctuary opened on their own.

Light poured in—not holy, not dramatic—just afternoon sun catching dust the way it always had.

I walked down the aisle alone.

Every step felt like stepping out of borrowed time.

At the threshold, I turned once and looked back.

The sanctuary was already changing.

The pulpit softened into a table.

The rows of chairs blurred.

The room was becoming something smaller.

Something truer.

A place where words would no longer be required to prove belief.

I stepped outside.

The doors closed.

The building exhaled.

I didn't lock it.

I didn't burn it.

I simply left it behind—

a husk I no longer needed to inhabit.

Outside, the pecan tree waited.

Its bark was split where the nail would one day go.

The sky did not darken.

The earth did not shake.

But something old finally loosened its grip.

Tomorrow would begin asking harder questions.

Chapter 6

The fire from the church followed me home, a weight in my chest as I picked up the shovel.

The backyard had grown over the spot years ago.

Azaleas.

St. Augustine grass.

The swing set Theo outgrew at seven.

I started under the pecan tree where the obituary had hung.

Elise watched from the porch, arms wrapped around herself, not speaking.

Lydia Grace sat on the steps with her knees to her chest, eighteen going on ancient.

Theo was at school.

I thanked God for small mercies.

The shovel hit metal at four feet down.

A rusted Folgers can, the kind Daddy used to bury fishing lures in.

I pried the lid off with shaking hands.

Inside—

One Polaroid of a girl I hadn't seen since 1987, smiling, eight weeks pregnant.

The clinic receipt—the original, not the burning copy Mercy Joy left.

A cashier's check made out to "cash" for $187.33—uncashed.

A single rusty sixteen-penny nail wrapped in a yellowed sonogram.

The sonogram had a name written in faded ink.

Mercy Joy Shepherdson.

My handwriting.

I sat in the hole and cried.

Elise came and sat on the edge of the dirt.

She didn't ask questions.

She just put her hand on my shoulder and let me sob until the sun went down.

When I could finally speak, I held up the sonogram.

"This is her," I said.

"This is who came to the living room."

Elise took it with trembling fingers.

She stared at it for a long time.

Then she did the thing I will never deserve.

She kissed the picture.

"She's beautiful," she murmured.

Something inside me fractured again.

Lydia Grace walked over, looked into the hole, and said the first words she'd spoken to me since her birthday.

"Dad, why is there only one nail?"

I couldn't answer.

Because I knew.

One nail for the girl.

One nail for the boy.

And one for me.

The hole stayed open.

Tomorrow was already waiting at the bottom.

Chapter 7

The abortion clinic had been a strip-mall salon for thirty years.

Google Maps knew that.

The city of Baton Rouge knew that.

But at 3:17 a.m., it stood there anyway.

Same cracked parking lot.

Same flickering pink sign that once read Women's Choice, half the letters dead.

Same rusted metal door I walked through at nineteen, thinking money could make a problem disappear.

I parked across the street and stared.

The building breathed.

The windows pulsed like lungs.

Each exhale smelled of antiseptic and fear.

I got out of the truck.

The asphalt was warm under my bare feet though the night was cold.

The door opened before I touched it.

Inside, the waiting room was 1987 again—orange plastic chairs, dog-eared magazines, a fish tank with one dead angelfish floating belly-up.

The receptionist desk was empty.

The clipboard wasn't.

My name was already there, written in my teenage hand.

Micah C. Shepherdson — 10:30 a.m. — Cash paid

I heard the doctor before I saw him.

Rubber soles on linoleum.

That squeak that never left my dreams.

He stepped out wearing green scrubs, paper mask pulled down, eyes bored and unaged.

Forty-nine forever.

"Running a little late, son," he said.

"We've been holding your spot."

I tried to step back.

The door was gone.

Just cinder-block wall where it used to be.

He pointed to the table.

Stirrups open.

Paper sheet crinkling.

"I'm not here for that," I said.

He smiled without warmth.

"You never left."

Then Mercy Joy stepped out from behind him.

Nineteen and fifty at the same time.

Belly round.

Dress alive with a soft glow.

She took my hand—skin warm.

"Come see what you paid for," she said.

She led me past the doctor into the procedure room.

The table was empty.

The trash can wasn't.

A red biohazard bag sat inside it, tied with a yellow ribbon—the same kind I used on Lydia Grace's birthday presents.

Mercy Joy knelt, untied it, and lifted out a tiny girl.

No bigger than my hand.

Umbilical cord still attached.

Eyes closed.

She placed the child in my arms.

It buckled my knees.

The baby opened her eyes.

They were mine.

She touched my cheek with a hand no bigger than a dime.

The room began to fold.

Mercy Joy leaned close.

“Take her home, Daddy—twenty-seven left.”

Then the world went white.

I woke in the parking lot at dawn.

The salon was gone again—boarded windows, weeds pushing through cracks.

I was holding something wrapped in a yellow ribbon.

I didn’t open it.

I turned toward the cemetery.

Chapter 8

Lydia Grace came home from her first college classes with a manila envelope and tears in her eyes.

She found me in the backyard, still kneeling in the hole I'd been digging since sunrise.

She didn't ask what I was doing.

She just handed me the envelope.

Inside was a single sheet of paper.

An ultrasound.

Eight weeks.

The name at the top read:

Lydia Grace Shepherdson — Patient

She was shaking.

"I'm keeping it," she said before I could speak.

"I'm not you."

The words hit harder than any fist.

I looked at the picture.

The baby was the exact size Mercy Joy had been when I paid to make her disappear.

I started crying so hard I couldn't see.

Lydia Grace knelt in the dirt beside me.

She took the ultrasound and placed it next to the yellow-ribbon bundle I still hadn't opened.

Then she did something I will never deserve.

She put her arms around me and murmured the same words Elise had used the day before.

"We're going to carry this together."

From the house, Theo's voice called out.

"Dad?

There's a little boy at the door asking for you."

I looked up.

Asher stood on the porch in his tornado-sky pajamas, eight years old, barefoot, smiling like he belonged there.

He waved.

In his other hand he held a tiny wooden cross made from pecan wood.

Lydia Grace saw him too.

Her mouth fell open.

Asher spoke without moving his lips.

"Hi, big sister.

I've been waiting to meet my niece."

Then he walked straight into the house like he'd lived there his whole life.

I looked at Lydia Grace.

She looked at me.

We both looked at the hole.

And for the first time in fifty years,

I started filling it back in.

Chapter 9

I preached my last sermon to empty chairs.

The church was locked.

The fire marshal had condemned the building after the baptistry miracle.

Yellow tape across every door.

But I still had a key.

I walked in at dawn carrying nothing but the yellow-ribbon bundle and the ultrasound Lydia Grace had left on my nightstand.

The cross behind the pulpit was still burning—blue flame, no smoke, no heat.

I stood where I had stood ten thousand Sundays and opened the only Bible I had left.

The one Mercy Joy had torn the page from.

I had no notes.

I just started talking to the empty chairs.

"Church," I said,

"I have been your pastor for thirty-nine years.

I have lied to you every single Sunday."

My voice echoed off the scorched walls.

"I stood here and preached grace while I paid to kill my own child.

I preached family while I buried a son I never let draw breath.

I preached resurrection while I lived like a dead man."

I laid the yellow-ribbon bundle on the pulpit.

It started bleeding light.

"I'm not here to ask forgiveness.

I'm here to give you back what was never mine."

I opened my wallet and poured every bill, every coin, every credit card onto the stage.

Then I took off my wedding ring—the one Elise put on my finger December 1, 2013—and laid it on top.

The ring started glowing.

I kept going.

"I resign.

I abdicate.

I repent in dust and ashes."

I got on my knees and poured the dirt from the backyard hole over my head.

It smelled like Mercy Joy and Asher and every prayer I never prayed.

The burning cross flared brighter.

Then the front doors opened.

The Pale Rider walked in, still wearing my father's face, and sat in the exact spot Daddy sat every Sunday when I was a boy.

He clapped once.

Slow.

Deliberate.

The sound cracked like a rifle shot.

"That's the first honest sermon you ever preached, son."

He stood up, walked to the stage, and picked up my wedding ring.

He held it to the light.

"Twenty-five days," he said.

"Clock's ticking."

Then he put the ring in his pocket and walked out.

The doors closed by themselves.

The cross kept burning.

I stayed on my knees until the sun went down.

Tomorrow was already walking down the aisle.

CHAPTER 10

Elise found me in the shower at 2 a.m., fully clothed under cold water, shaking so hard the tiles rattled.

She stepped in without a word—shoes and all—and wrapped her arms around me until the storm inside quieted.

When the water finally ran clear of my tears, she turned it off and led me to our bed like I was the child and she the mother who had never stopped carrying me.

We lay there soaked and shivering, staring at the ceiling where shadows danced like ghosts waiting for permission to leave.

I whispered,

"I don't know how to be the man you married anymore."

She rolled over, placed her hand over the place Mercy Joy had pressed, and said,

"Then let's remember who we were the night we said yes."

She kissed my cheek.

Not the careful kiss of habit.

The kiss of two people who had just survived a shipwreck and found dry land in each other again.

We did not make love like the world calls it.

I told her everything while our bodies spoke the language we had forgotten we knew.

Every secret.

Every child.

Every grave.

She answered with forgiveness that felt like resurrection.

When I wept Mercy Joy's name into her neck, she held me tighter and breathed,

"She's ours now."

When she wept mine into my chest, I felt the years of delayed truth begin to give way to something earned.

Afterward, we lay tangled in the ruins of who we used to be, breathing the same air for the first time in decades.

She took my hand and placed it on her belly—flat, familiar, holy.

"I stopped the pill last year," she said.

"I wanted one more miracle before the clock ran out.

I never told you because I was afraid you'd say we were too old."

The tears came again, different now—lighter, almost clean.

She kissed them away.

“Twenty-four days,” she murmured.

“Whatever time we have left, we’re going to spend it making room for every child we lost.”

Outside the window, the pecan tree began to glow, soft and steady, like a night-light left on for children who were finally coming home.

Tomorrow could wait one more night.

We had graves to unmake

and a marriage to resurrect.

The house had never felt more like a temple.

And for the first time since 1987,

I fell asleep without owing anyone a tomorrow.

Chapter 11

Asher came to me at dawn.

He was sitting on the foot of our bed in his tornado-sky pajamas, legs swinging like he was waiting for pancakes.

Elise was still asleep, one hand resting on the place where new life might already be knitting itself together.

Asher put a finger to his lips and motioned for me to follow.

I slipped out of bed and walked behind him down the hallway.

He led me to the spare room we never finished—the one that was supposed to be a nursery once, then a study, then just a graveyard for boxes.

The door opened by itself.

Inside, the walls were gone.

It was a field at night.

Thousands of children stood in perfect rows, barefoot, glowing faintly.

Every age.

Every shade of skin.

Every eye fixed on me.

Asher walked to the front and turned.

He raised his small hand and began to speak.

But he didn't use English.

He spoke their names.

One after another, rapid fire, like wind through wheat.

Names I had never heard but somehow knew.

Every child aborted in our parish the year I paid for one.

Every syllable hit me like a hammer on an anvil.

My knees buckled.

I fell face-down in the dirt that smelled like hospital floors and clinic parking lots.

Asher kept speaking.

The names became a river.

The river became a roar.

Then he stopped.

Silence so complete I could hear my own heart trying to hide.

Asher knelt beside me and placed his hand on the back of my neck.

His touch burned like mercy.

"Stand up, Daddy," he whispered.

"They waited fifty years for you to learn how to pray for them."

I stood.

Every child took one step forward.

Then, in perfect unison, they spoke a single sentence in a thousand voices:

"We forgive you.

Now forgive yourself."

The field vanished.

I was back in the spare room.

The boxes were gone.

The walls were bare and clean.

Asher was gone.

But on the floor lay a single white candle, still burning, no wax, no wick.

Tomorrow was already learning the next name.

Chapter 12

April Fool's Day.

I drove to the cemetery where the girl from 1987 was buried.

Her name was Sarah Elizabeth Cole.

She died in a car wreck six months after the clinic.

I never went to the funeral.

The grave was overgrown, marker cracked, forgotten.

I brought a shovel and the white candle that never went out.

I started digging.

At three feet down I found it.

A small cedar box she had buried the day before she died.

Inside—

A letter addressed to me in her nineteen-year-old handwriting.

A tiny pair of knitted booties.

A Polaroid of her holding the ultrasound, smiling through tears.

The letter was one page.

Micah,

If you ever read this, it means you finally grew a spine.

I forgave you the day I signed the form.

I just wanted you to know the baby had a name.

We were going to call her Hope.

I hope you find some.

See you on the other side.

—Sarah

I sat in the hole and read it until the paper disintegrated from my tears.

When I looked up, she was standing at the edge of the grave.

Nineteen years old.

Alive.

Whole.

She smiled the way Mercy Joy smiled—like she had never been broken.

She reached down and helped me climb out.

Then she did the thing that finished killing the old me.

She hugged me.

Not a ghost hug.

A real one.

Flesh and bone and forgiveness that had weight.

“I kept my promise,” she whispered into my shoulder.

“Now keep yours.”

She stepped back, turned, and walked into the sunrise.

The grave filled itself.

The marker was new, shining, engraved:

SARAH ELIZABETH COLE

and

HOPE

Beloved mother and daughter

Forgiven and forgiving

The candle in my hand went out for the first time.

Chapter 13

I wrote the letters at the kitchen table while the house slept.

Four envelopes.

Four names written in shaking ink.

Elise

Lydia Grace

Theo

Mercy Joy & Asher

I didn't begin with If you're reading this, I'm dead.

I began with the only words that still felt honest.

I'm sorry.

I love you.

Thank you.

Forgive me.

I told Elise everything I had never dared say in the light.

How her yes on December 1, 2013, was the first mercy I didn't refuse.

How every morning I woke up beside her felt like stolen grace.

I told Lydia Grace she saved my life the day she refused to become me.

I told her the child inside her was already braver than I had ever been.

I told Theo his laughter was the only sound that ever drowned out the clinic's silence.

I told him I was proud of the man he was becoming while I was still learning to be his father.

I told Mercy Joy and Asher that I had finally learned their names by heart.

That I would spend whatever days I had left speaking them like prayers.

I sealed each envelope with wax and the pecan-wood cross Asher had carved.

Then I laid them on the table in a careful row.

I left a note on top.

Open these the day I disappear.

Not before.

Not after.

The day the story starts.

I went outside and sat beneath the tree that had worn my obituary.

The nail hole was still there, leaking light.

Chapter 14

e didn't go to church.

There was no church left to go to.

Instead we gathered in the living room at dusk—Elise, Lydia Grace, Theo, and me.

I filled a basin with water that burned without consuming.

I took off my shoes.

I knelt in front of Elise first.

She tried to pull away.

I held her feet like they were holy.

I washed twenty-three years of hidden years off her skin.

I kissed the scars from carrying children I never deserved.

She wept without sound.

Then Lydia Grace.

Eighteen years old and already braver than I ever was.

I washed the feet that would soon walk hospital halls for a different reason.

She let me.

Then Theo.

Eleven years old, trying so hard to be a man.

I washed the dirt from playgrounds and treehouses and the places boys go when their fathers disappear into graves they dug themselves.

He didn't cry until I kissed the top of his foot and murmured,

"I'm still here, son.

And I'm not leaving until I've earned the right to stay."

When I finished, Lydia Grace filled the basin again.

She knelt in front of me.

One by one they washed my feet.

The water confessed, then bled, then cleared.

When Theo poured it over my heels, the cracks in the floor began to glow.

No words were needed.

We didn't need to.

The veil was tearing again, this time in our living room.

The days bled on.

Chapter 15

I woke nailed to a tree.

Not the pecan tree.

A rough-hewn cross stood in the middle of our backyard, built from the same lumber I used for Lydia Grace's treehouse.

I was upright, wrists and feet pierced with the two remaining sixteen-penny nails.

But I was not alone.

Asher stood before me—older now—full-grown, radiant with the gravity of someone who had passed through death and refused to stay.

He wore a simple white robe.

Barefoot.

Unmarked.

In his hands he held a crown of pecan thorns.

He set it on my head.

Not gently.

Blood ran into my eyes.

He murmured the words he had every right to say—the words I had spent fifty years refusing to hear.

“Father, forgive him.

He doesn’t know what he’s doing.”

Then he stepped back.

Mercy Joy stood beside him, nineteen and fifty at once.

Her belly was flat now.

Her eyes burned.

She held the yellow-ribbon bundle—no longer small.

She unwrapped it.

Inside was the child I paid to erase, now full-term, alive, breathing.

Mercy Joy placed her in my nailed arms.

It bowed me.

The baby opened her eyes and looked at me.

She smiled.

She reached up with a hand the size of a dime and touched the blood at my brow.

Where she touched me, the wound closed.

The sky darkened at noon.

Thunder rolled.

Elise, Lydia Grace, and Theo ran into the yard.

They saw me on the cross.

They did not scream.

They knelt.

Lydia Grace—heavy with child—laid her hand on the wood.

Theo rested his head against my foot.

Elise stood beneath me, hand pressed to the wood as if feeling for a pulse.

She spoke the words that ended fifty years of silence.

"It is finished."

The sky waited.

Even the blood waited.

The nails released.

I fell into their arms.

The cross broke down into sawdust.

Nineteen days.

I had nineteen days to learn how to die

after the lie I lived under had finally died.

Tomorrow would be the day the King rested in the tomb.

I finally understood why.

Some graves must stay shut for three days

so the world can learn the difference

between dead

and done.

Chapter 16

The Pale Rider came at dusk.

He rode straight through the front door without opening it.

The house went cold.

He stood in the living room wearing my father's face, but the eyes were older now—older than creation, older than sin.

He carried no whip.

No scroll.

Only my wedding ring in his open palm.

He laid it on the coffee table next to the four sealed letters.

Then he spoke, and the walls trembled.

"The offer stands one more day," he said.

"Die tonight.

Clean slate.

The timeline stays intact.

Elise keeps her husband.

Lydia Grace keeps her father.

Theo keeps his childhood.

Mercy Joy and Asher stay forgiven but forgotten.

No one else ever has to know."

He placed a single nail on top of the ring.

One nail.

For me.

I looked at Elise.

She was crying, but her eyes were steady.

I looked at Lydia Grace, hand on her belly.

I looked at Theo, trying so hard not to be afraid.

I looked at the empty place where Asher and Mercy Joy usually stood.

They didn't appear.

The Rider waited.

The silence was a tomb.

I picked up the nail.

I walked to the backyard.

I drove it into the pecan tree myself, right through the scar where my obituary had hung.

Then I turned to him.

“No,” I said.

The Rider smiled for the first time.

It was not kind.

“Then tomorrow the borrowed days start collapsing,” he said.

“Every mercy you refused will come due.

Every child you buried will rise.

And you will watch the ones you love pay the interest.”

He mounted up.

The horse reared.

They rode straight through the wall and were gone.

The nail in the tree began to bleed light.

Eighteen days left—

to choose between dying clean

and living long enough to watch everything I love burn

so that nothing I love would ever have to burn again.

I walked back inside.

Elise was waiting.

She took my hand—the one that had just refused the easy death.

“Whatever comes,” she said,

“we carry it together.”

Outside, the pecan tree started to grow nails like fruit.

Tomorrow the dead would begin to wake.

Chapter 17

I woke thirty-four years younger.

The ceiling above me was the water-stained popcorn of the apartment I rented in 2003—the year I thought I had outrun my past.

My hands were smooth.

No arthritis.

No ring.

I sat up too fast.

The room tilted.

On the nightstand lay a Polaroid I had burned in 2009.

Me at nineteen, arm around Sarah Elizabeth Cole, both of us smiling like the future was ours.

The date on the photo was three days from now.

I crossed the room and faced the mirror.

The man who signed the clinic form stared back.

The face was young.

The eyes were not.

They carried fifty years I hadn't lived yet.

Thirty-three—

the age Jesus died.

The age I was meant to die.

I had been brought back to the day I wasted most.

One day.

I pulled on the clothes hanging in the closet—jeans that fit, a T-shirt untouched by regret.

My phone buzzed.

A number I hadn't saved.

Elise.

We hadn't met yet.

The message was short.

Coffee?

I'm outside.

I went to the window.

She leaned against a red Honda Civic, hair shorter than I remembered, twenty-four years old, smiling like the world hadn't taught her how to brace for pain.

Lydia Grace was eight years away.

Theo was nineteen.

Mercy Joy and Asher still belonged to a future I could erase.

One choice stood between everything that had been

and everything that could still be.

Downstairs—or away.

The Pale Rider sat on the hood of my truck thirty-three feet below, wearing my younger face.

He lifted a single nail in greeting.

The clock read 6:00 a.m.

I had until 3:00 p.m.—the hour I would die—to decide which life would survive.

I opened the door.

Tomorrow was already here, wearing yesterday's clothes.

Chapter 18

I said no.

I shut the apartment door, walked past Elise without looking back, climbed into my truck, and drove.

I chose the borrowed timeline.

I chose the family.

I chose the graves.

The moment the truck hit the highway, my sky tore open.

Not the world's sky—

mine.

A private apocalypse, visible only to the man who had just refused the mercy of forgetting.

The windshield thinned into a veil.

Through it poured light the color of birth and blood and fire.

The dead did not rise from Louisiana soil.

They rose from me.

Mercy Joy stood in the middle of the road—full-term, alive—arms open, blocking my path.

Asher stood beside her, eleven now, Theo's age, holding Theo's hand.

And behind them were no multitudes, no unnamed masses—

only the two I buried.

But two was enough to unmake a lifetime.

Their gaze stopped the truck dead.

The engine died.

The radio screamed my name in the voice of every prayer I never prayed.

Then the ground beneath the truck opened.

Not the earth.

My earth.

The fault line I had lived on since 1987.

Hands reached up—my own hands, nineteen years old, the ones that signed the form, the ones that paid the bill, the ones that walked away.

They were pulling me down to make room for the children coming up.

I got out of the truck.

Mercy Joy walked toward me, glowing with a forgiveness I had never earned.

She placed her hand on my chest, right where she had pressed the first time.

"You chose us," she said.

Her voice was two mothers forgiving at once.

The sky above me kept tearing, a wound reopening, a veil refusing to stay mended.

I fell to my knees on asphalt that felt like the clinic floor.

The children surrounded me.

Not to condemn—

to carry.

Asher knelt and whispered,

"Sixteen days, Daddy.

The borrowed days are collapsing.

But the real ones are just beginning."

Then the vision folded.

The highway was empty again.

The truck started on its own.

I was sixty-seven, scarred, my wedding ring back on my finger.

But the receipt in my pocket

was now warm

and wet

with something that smelled

like the edge of mercy.

CHAPTER 19

I sat on the back-porch steps at dawn, coffee gone cold, staring at the pecan tree that had carried so many nails.

Something shifted in the air — not a wind, but a pressure, like the house itself inhaling.

I felt it before I understood it: a weight settling around my temples, faint pulses syncing with heartbeats that weren't only mine.

Not a crown of light or woven strands.

Just the sense of lives pressing close — the children whose tomorrows I had interrupted, their rhythms brushing against my own.

Twelve faint echoes, maybe more, maybe fewer.

I couldn't count them.

They didn't speak.

They simply rested there, undeniable but quiet, the way grief sometimes arrives without announcement.

Elise opened the back door and saw me sitting motionless, eyes closed, hands open on my knees.

She didn't ask what I saw or felt.

She walked down the steps and stood behind me, hands on my shoulders.

Theo and Lydia Grace followed a moment later, drawn by the same silence.

They formed a loose circle around me.

No one touched the places where the pulses seemed strongest.

We just stood together until the morning light strengthened and the weight eased — not gone, but shared.

Twenty-eight heartbeats in one backyard, maybe.

Or only four.

I couldn't tell anymore.

And that was mercy enough.

Chapter 20

I drove to the condemned church parking lot at noon alone.

Yellow tape flapped in the breeze.

I walked to the spot where the baptistry had once burned without consuming and stood there with the single nail I'd pulled from the pecan tree.

No hammer.

No ritual.

Just the cracked asphalt and the heat rising off it.

I spoke to the thing I'd carried longest.

Not loudly.

"Come out."

The words felt small against the empty building.

Nothing answered.

I pressed the nail against my left palm until blood welled.

The pain was immediate, ordinary.

The nineteen-year-old version of me didn't step out of my shadow.

He was just there suddenly, in my mind's eye — cocky grin, blood already on his hands from years ago.

He didn't speak the old lies aloud.

I heard them anyway.

It was just a clump of cells.

You were too young.

God forgives anyway.

I named the children instead, quietly.

Mercy Joy.

Asher.

Hope.

The child Elise lost.

One by one, the lies thinned.

The boy in my mind looked at me for a long moment, eyes finally meeting mine.

Then he faded — not dramatically, not into tar or smoke.

He simply wasn't there anymore.

The nail dropped from my hand.

The wound closed slowly, the way cuts do when you're old and the blood moves slower.

I stood there until the sun shifted.

When I got home that evening, Elise brought me coffee on the back steps and sat beside me.

She noticed the healing cut on my palm but didn't ask.

We listened to the crickets start up.

The silence felt clean for the first time in decades.

Fourteen days.

Chapter 21

Nothing happened.
No earthquakes.
No angels descending.
No trumpet blasts.

Just the ordinary Sunday sounds of a Louisiana spring: birds arguing, a lawnmower two streets over, Theo laughing at cartoons in the living room.

I woke expecting fire.

Instead I got sunrise through the bedroom window and Elise's hand on my chest, feeling for the heartbeat she had guarded for twenty-three years.

She opened her eyes.
"You're still here," she breathed.

I started crying before I could stop myself.

She pulled me close like I was the child.

We stayed in bed until the light turned gold.

Later, Lydia Grace made cross-shaped pancakes because that's what you do when you're eighteen and pregnant and your father might die any day.

Theo set the table without being asked.

We ate in silence that felt like worship.

No one mentioned the weight at dawn, the nails, the children who visited in the night.

When the plates were empty, Lydia Grace reached for my hand.
"Grandpa," she said—for the first time—
"the baby kicked during the blessing."

I put my palm on her belly.

I felt it.

A tiny foot pressing against the wall of the womb, saying hello.

A faint heartbeat answered from somewhere I could not see.

The loudest resurrections, I was learning,
are the ones that happen around kitchen tables
when nobody is watching.

Chapter 22

The Pale Rider returned at dusk.

He did not ride this time.

He walked up the driveway barefoot, wearing my face the way I looked in photographs from the year I believed I had it all together.

Same height.

Same gray at the temples.

Same tired eyes.

Only the eyes were older than sin.

He stopped ten feet away.

Elise, Lydia Grace, and Theo stood behind me on the porch.

He looked at them, then at me.

"You look like hell," he said.

I laughed before I could stop myself.

He smiled the way I used to smile when I still believed I could outrun consequence.

"I'm tired, Micah," he said.

"Carrying your borrowed days is heavy."

He reached into his pocket and pulled out the wedding ring he had taken from the pulpit.

He held it out.

"One last chance," he said.

"Put it on.

Die tonight.

Clean.

Quiet.

The crown dissolves.

The nails rust.

The timeline heals."

He waited.

The ring caught the last light of the day and threw it back like fire.

I looked at Elise.

She was crying, but her hand found mine.

I looked at Lydia Grace, hand on her belly.

I looked at Theo, trying so hard to be brave.

I looked at the place where Mercy Joy and Asher usually stood.

They were there.

Visible to all of us now.

Mercy Joy nodded once.

Asher smiled—the easy, weightless smile of a child who has already forgiven everything.

I turned back to the Rider.

I took the ring from his hand.

I slipped it onto my finger again where it had always belonged.

Then I stepped forward and hugged the man wearing my face.

He went rigid.

I murmured into his ear the only thing left to say.

"Thank you for carrying me this far.

But I'm done borrowing."

I stepped back.

The Rider aged fifty years in a single breath.

Skin sagged.

Hair whitened.

Eyes hollowed.

He looked suddenly, unbearably old.

He nodded once.

Then he turned and walked down the driveway.

His footprints filled with light and stayed glowing long after he was gone.

We stayed on the porch long after his glowing footprints faded.

Elise's hand in mine.

Lydia Grace's head on my shoulder, her belly pressing warm against my side.

Theo curled against my leg like he was five again.

No one moved to go inside.

The pecan tree stood dark against the sky, nails glinting like stars caught in its branches.

I felt the weight of every tomorrow I'd refused to borrow settle into something solid.

Something earned.

Elise finally breathed, "Bed?"

I nodded.

We went in together, four shadows becoming one in the doorway.

Twelve days.

I had twelve days to finish becoming the man

the Rider had carried for me all these years.

Tomorrow the children would start asking for their father back

in ways the world had never seen.

Chapter 23

Asher came to me at dawn in the garage while I was finally fixing the shelf I'd promised Theo years ago.

He was eight again, barefoot in his tornado-sky pajamas, holding nothing.

He didn't speak.

He just took my hand and led me out back, past the pecan tree, down to the bayou where the cypress knees rose like old witnesses.

We walked into the water together.

It was cold enough to remind me I was still breathing.

He turned to face me.

No raised hands.

No formal words.

He simply looked at me the way children do when they've waited long enough.

I went under on my own — not pushed, just surrendering to the weight I carried.

Under the surface everything went quiet.

I saw open places where graves should have been.

Empty.

Not dramatic.

Just empty.

When I came up, Asher was still there, water to his waist, watching.

He didn't grow taller.

He didn't speak welcome.

He just nodded once, the way a son does when his father finally shows up.

We walked out together.

The morning light caught the drops on his pajamas and made them ordinary again.

I carried no newborn version of myself.

Only the sense that something old had stayed under the water.

Eleven days.

Chapter 24

Mercy Joy came at midnight.

I was awake beside sleeping Elise when the room grew faintly warmer, like someone had left a candle burning somewhere out of sight.

She stood at the foot of the bed — her dress the soft color of banked coals.

She didn't lean over.

She didn't kiss my cheek.

She simply looked at me for a long moment, eyes holding everything we hadn't said in life.

Then she placed her hand over her heart and nodded once.

The warmth settled in my chest.

Just warmth.

Enough to remind me she had forgiven long before I asked.

She stepped back into the shadows.

Elise stirred, opened her eyes, and saw nothing but me awake.

She reached for my hand under the covers.

We lay there until sleep returned.

Outside, the pecan tree dropped one nail in the dark.

I heard it hit the ground soft as a sigh.

Ten days.

Chapter 25

Mercy Joy left on a Tuesday.

She came to breakfast like any other morning, barefoot, fire-dress the soft color of sunrise on water.

Elise was making biscuits.

Lydia Grace was humming to the baby that kicked inside her.

Theo was sneaking extra bacon.

Mercy Joy sat at the table in the empty chair that had always been hers.

No one was surprised to see her.

She looked at me with fifty-year-old eyes and nineteen-year-old hope.

"It's time, Daddy," she said.

I knew what she meant.

I pushed my plate away.

Elise turned off the stove without a word.

We all walked outside together.

The pecan tree had dropped every nail but one.

Mercy Joy stood beneath it.

She reached up and took the last nail in her small hand.

Then she did the thing I had waited fifty years for

and never deserved.

She forgave me out loud.

In front of my wife and my children

and the Louisiana morning.

“I love you,” she said.

“I always did.

You kept me waiting a long time,

but you finally came.”

She kissed my cheek.

Her lips left a scar shaped like mercy.

Then she walked to the edge of the yard where the light was thickest.

She turned once.

She smiled the way only forgiven children can.

And stepped through.

The air closed behind her like water.

The last nail fell from the tree

and landed soft as forgiveness.

The rest of that Tuesday passed as slow as grief.

I walked the yard three times, fingertips brushing the place on my cheek where her kiss had burned mercy into my skin.

The scar was already cooling into something I could carry.

Elise found me under the tree.

She didn't speak.

She just slipped her arm around my waist and leaned her head against my chest.

We stood there until the light shifted.

Inside, Lydia Grace was humming again, low and steady, to the baby that kicked answers back.

I closed my eyes and let the sound fill the place Mercy Joy had left empty.

It fit.

Nine days.

I had nine days to learn how to live without the daughter

who taught me how to be a father

before the next child asked to leave.

Chapter 26

Asher left on a Wednesday.

He found me in the garage, fixing the same shelf I had promised Theo I'd fix for three years.

He was eight again—tornado-sky pajamas, barefoot—carrying the wooden cross he had carved from pecan wood.

He climbed onto the workbench and sat swinging his legs.

"I'm ready, Daddy," he said.

I put down the hammer.

I knew.

I picked him up—

light as forgiveness,

heavy as every bedtime I never read.

We walked to the backyard.

The hole I had dug and filled and dug again was waiting.

Only now it was lined with the yellow ribbon that had never burned.

Asher lay down in it like it was the comfiest bed in the world.

He looked up at me with eyes that had already seen tomorrow.

"Bury me right this time," he whispered.

I started crying so hard I couldn't see.

Elise, Lydia Grace, and Theo stood behind me.

Lydia Grace was singing the lullaby I never sang to him.

I covered him with dirt, one handful at a time.

Each handful felt like putting my heart back where it belonged.

When the last scoop fell, a pecan sprout pushed through the soil.

Green.

Alive.

Bearing tiny fruit.

Asher's voice came from inside the tree, small and perfect:

"See you soon, Daddy.

Tell Theo I'm proud of him."

The sprout grew six inches while we watched.

CHAPTER 27

The clinic called me at 6:00 a.m.

The same number from 1987.

Same recorded voice, now fifty years older and still bored.

"Mr. Shepherdson, your appointment is today at ten thirty.

Please do not be late."

I hung up before the message finished.

Elise was already awake.

She handed me the keys without a word.

Lydia Grace and Theo stood in the hallway, eyes wide, knowing.

I drove alone.

The strip-mall nail salon was gone again.

In its place stood the clinic exactly as it looked the day I paid.

Pink sign flickering.

Parking lot cracked.

Same rusted door.

It was waiting.

I walked in.

The waiting room was empty except for one chair.

Mine.

The clipboard was on it.

My name was already written.

I signed nothing.

The door to the procedure room opened by itself.

I walked through.

The table was ready.

Stirrups cold.

Paper crinkling like accusation.

But no doctor.

Only Mercy Joy and Asher standing at the foot.

Mercy Joy, full-grown, gentle fire.

Asher, eleven, holding the wooden cross.

They did not speak.

They simply looked at me the way children look at fathers who finally came home.

I understood.

I took off my shoes.

I lay down on the table voluntarily.

Asher placed the pecan-wood cross on my chest.

Mercy Joy took my hand.

The room filled with light—soft, womb-colored.

I felt the old man die on that table.

Not with violence.

With surrender.

When the light faded, the clinic was gone.

I was lying in the backyard, under the pecan tree that now bore a single perfect blossom.

CHAPTER 28

They came at twilight.

Three men on foot, walking up the driveway like they had nowhere else to be.

Old.

Weathered.

Carrying nothing but plain tools.

The first carried a small box that glowed like something alive.

The second, a jar of oil that smelled like birth and burial at once.

The third, a hammer.

They stopped ten feet away.

Elise, Lydia Grace, and Theo stood behind me on the porch.

The man with the hammer spoke first.

"We heard there was a man here who finally learned to die," he said.

His voice was gravel and grace.

I stepped forward.

The man with the glowing box opened it.

Inside was a single nail, warmed by a fire older than the world.

The man with the oil poured a single drop on the nail.

It hissed like water on embers.

Then he handed me the hammer.

I knew what came next.

I walked to the pecan tree.

I placed the nail against the trunk, right where my obituary had hung.

I raised the hammer.

Elise started to cry.

Lydia Grace put her hand on her belly.

Theo whispered, "Do it, Grandpa."

I drove the nail home.

Not into wood.

Into every lie I ever told.

Every mercy I ever refused.

Every child I ever buried.

The tree split open with a sound like the veil tearing again.

Light poured out.

Not blinding.

Healing.

The three men nodded once.

Then they turned and walked back down the driveway.

Their footprints filled with water that reflected a sky I had never seen before.

Chapter 29

They came at dawn.

Not in visions.

Not as ghosts.

Not as resurrected bodies stepping out of graves.

They came the way the dead and the wounded always come—

through the door of memory

once you finally stop locking it.

I stepped onto the porch barefoot.

They were already there, standing quietly across the yard.

Not their bodies—

the remembered faces.

The versions of them I had carried for decades.

The versions I had wounded.

Sarah Elizabeth Cole

(fifty-seven in the world I never lived to see;

nineteen forever in the one where I left her alone).

The doctor from 1987

(no scrubs, just the tired eyes I never let myself meet).

The woman I betrayed Elise with

(older now, wiser, holding nothing but her own peace).

The pastor whose trust I chipped away.

The friend I abandoned.

The stranger in the clinic parking lot I never forgot.

Each one stood exactly as I remembered them—

and exactly as they needed to be remembered.

No anger.

No accusation.

Just the quiet gravity of people who had waited

for me to stop running.

Elise stepped onto the porch beside me.

Lydia Grace and Theo came too—silent, steady, bearing witness.

Sarah stepped forward first.

She didn't speak.

She simply hugged me—

not the real Sarah,

but the Sarah I had carried in shame for fifty years.

When she stepped back, a folded letter remained in my hand—

the one she wrote the day she forgave me

and never gave me.

One by one they came.

Each placed something in my hands.

A photograph.

A hospital bracelet.

A knitted bootie.

A line from a whispered prayer.

A forgiveness they had already offered long ago

but I had never received.

Each said the same three words,

in voices only I could hear:

"I forgive you."

When the last stepped back,

the offerings lay scattered across the grass

like the pieces of my old life

finally allowed to breathe.

The crown dissolved into soft light

and lifted from my head,

settling over the offerings like a mantle.

I fell to my knees.

CHAPTER 30

Asher came at dusk carrying nothing.

He was eight, then older, then eight again—the way children appear in dreams when time no longer matters.

He stopped beneath the pecan tree, now healed and heavy with summer leaf though the calendar said April.

He looked up at me.

"It's time, Daddy."

I knew.

I walked to the tree alone.

No three forged spikes.

Just the single nail I'd carried since the parking lot.

I pressed it against the trunk where the scar had been.

I didn't drive it home.

I simply held it there until the wood warmed beneath my palm.

The air thinned.

The yard fell away quietly.

I found myself standing in a room I recognized—not the clinic, but the hollow place I'd lived inside for fifty years.

It was full of light, not blinding.

The children were there—Mercy Joy, Asher, Hope, the ones Elise and I lost.

They weren't laughing loudly.

They weren't gathered in perfect rows.

They were just present, whole, waiting without hurry.

Asher stepped forward.

He didn't place anything in my nailed hands.

He simply took them—scarred palms up—and held them.

The child I finally became wasn't newborn in my arms.

It was standing beside me, small but steady, looking up with my own eyes.

Four days.

I had four days to finish learning how to hold that child's hand

and walk forward without letting go.

The room held us all.

No one was missing.

Tomorrow I would die at three o'clock.

And that would be enough.

CHAPTER 31

I died at three o'clock in the afternoon.

There was no darkness over the earth.

No earthquake.

No veil tearing that anyone else could see

Only the quiet of a Louisiana spring Friday

and the sound of Elise breathing beside me on the couch

where we had fallen asleep holding hands.

I had asked them not to call an ambulance.

I had asked them to let me go at home.

Lydia Grace sat on the floor, head against my knee,

one hand on her belly,

counting kicks like rosary beads.

Theo lay across my feet

the way he did when he was five and afraid of storms.

Asher and Mercy Joy were not visible,

but I felt them the way you feel warmth

from a fire you can no longer see.

At 2:58 the pain stopped.

At 2:59 I looked at Elise.

She was crying,

but smiling the way she smiled the day Lydia Grace was born.

I tried to speak.

Only one word came.

"Home."

At 3:00 exactly, I closed my eyes.

I did not see a tunnel.

I did not see a light.

I saw the pecan tree in full summer leaf,

and beneath it every child I had ever carried,

waiting.

Mercy Joy took my left hand.

Asher took my right.

I felt the child I had finally become

standing beside me, small but steady,

hand slipping into mine.

I took one more breath that belonged to this borrowed timeline.

Then I let it go.

There was no sound.

Only the soft click of a door closing

and the gentler opening of another.

Only three days remained in the story—

but none left in the dying.

Tomorrow the tomb would be empty,

and the resurrection would be so quiet

only the people who loved me most

would ever notice I was gone.

And that was enough.

Chapter 32

I woke inside the tomb that had been built for someone else.

Not a cave.
Not a grave.
Just the hollow place inside my own chest
where the old man used to live.

The stone was already rolled away.

I stepped out carrying nothing.

Mercy Joy and Asher were waiting.

Mercy Joy, full-grown,
fire now quiet as candlelight.

Asher, steady and young at once,
barefoot,
smiling like the storm had passed.

They did not speak.
They simply took my hands.

The child I had finally become
walked forward from the light,

small but steady,
and slipped his hand into mine.

We walked.
Not up.
Not out.
Forward.

The backyard was the same
and not the same.

The pecan tree stood in full summer leaf
though it was only April.

Elise was on the porch swing,
older than yesterday,
younger than sorrow.

Lydia Grace sat beside her, belly round, rocking gently.

Theo ran across the grass and stopped when he saw us.

He looked at Asher.
Then at me.
Then at the child beside me.

He understood.

He walked straight to Asher
and hugged him like a brother
he had always known was coming home.

Lydia Grace stood.
Tears,
but no surprise.

She kissed Mercy Joy on both cheeks
the way mothers greet daughters
they never got to raise.

Elise opened her arms.

I walked to her.

She took me close.

The child stood beside us, hand still in mine.

We sat on the swing together.

Two days now—
time enough, perhaps,
to learn how to live
as a man who had finally died right.

Tomorrow the story would end
and begin again
in the only way resurrections ever do:
quietly,
in the arms of the people
who never stopped waiting.

Chapter 35

The resurrection that was never supposed to happen

still happened.

There was no earthquake.

No trumpet.

No cosmic announcement.

Just breakfast.

Elise made biscuits.

Lydia Grace poured milk.

Theo set an extra plate

he no longer needed.

We sat around the table

that had always been big enough

and suddenly was.

Mercy Joy passed the butter.

Asher stole a piece of bacon
and grinned like forgiveness.
The child beside me—
no longer newborn,
no longer me—
reached for a biscuit
with perfect, tiny hands.
Outside, the pecan tree dropped one final nail.
It struck the ground
and bloomed into a thousand white flowers
that smelled like mercy
and tomorrow.
I looked around the table
at every child I had ever carried
and every child who had ever carried me.
Then I did the only thing left to do.
I spoke their names aloud
for the first time in front of the world
and meant every syllable.

Mercy Joy.

Asher.

Hope.

The twelve.

The child Elise lost.

The child Lydia Grace carried.

The child I finally became.

When the last name left my mouth,

the veil that had torn in my living room fifty years earlier

mended itself with light.

The borrowed timeline ended.

The real one began.

I was old.

I was new.

I was finished

and just getting started.

I looked at Elise across the table.

She smiled the way she smiled

the first morning she ever made me coffee

and the last morning she ever would.

I looked at Lydia Grace, Theo, Mercy Joy, Asher,

and the child who was no longer me

but would always be mine.

Then I said the only words still worth saying:

"Thank you

for letting me come home."

Outside, the pecan tree kept blooming.

Inside, the Kingdom was at hand,

and nobody was missing anymore.

This is the end.

And the beginning.

Epilogue

I know what I've written.
I didn't write it to win permission.
I didn't write it to soften the truth.

I wrote it to refuse the lie—
so tomorrow could finally start without the man I used to be.

Night Light

Click goes the night light
and the room exhales into dark—
not the grave-dark that swallows sound,
but the gentle kind that waits
for children to come home.

Somewhere the pecan tree
lets fall its final nail
without a whisper,
and the scar in the bark
closes like a mouth
finishing a prayer.

Tomorrow rises
without the man I used to be.
The table is set.
The biscuits are warm.
Everyone is here.

The Widening Witness

If this story has marked you, the witness widens in two companion works:

The Acceptable Cannon (July 2026)
Twelve Days Back (November 2026)

One quiet arc.
https://learningengineeredpublishing.com/co-shepherdso

www.ingramcontent.com/pod-product-compliance
Lightning Source LLC
LaVergne TN
LVHW010933110826
845149LV00013B/2581

* 9 7 8 1 9 6 5 7 4 1 6 6 5 *

Table of Contents

How to Use This Book 4
About Us 5
Introduction 6
Chapter 1: Choose Your Character 17
Chapter 2: Level Up Your Stats 25
Chapter 3: Building Habits Through Daily Quests 33
Chapter 4: Game Settings - Customizing Your Difficulty 43
Chapter 5: Gaining Experience Points (XP) and Reward Systems . 56
Chapter 6: Overcoming Obstacles and Boss Battles 65
Chapter 7: Multiplayer Mode — Building Your Party and Crushing Bosses Together 74
Chapter 8: The Feedback Loop - Your Life's HUD 85
Chapter 9: Leveling Up Your Skill Tree — Advanced Progress Systems 99
Chapter 10: Save Points and Backup Files - Recovery Systems .. 109
Chapter 11: Adapting to New Levels and Life Stages 121
Chapter 12: Continuous Learning and Innovation 129
Conclusion: Your Life, Your Game, Your Legacy 137
About the Authors 144

How to Use This Book

Welcome to *Gamify Your Life for Success: Level Up Your Goals, Habits, and Mindset*! This isn't just another motivational book; it's a game guide for the greatest adventure of all—your life. Whether you're a hardcore gamer, a casual card player, or someone who hasn't touched a joystick since the Atari days, this book is designed to help you level up your goals, habits, and mindset using the power of gamification.

Here's how to get the most out of it:

1. **Read It Like a Quest Log:** Each chapter is a quest, packed with actionable tips, examples, and exercises. Treat them as steps in your own epic campaign.

2. **Complete the Challenges:** At the end of many chapters, you'll find exercises or tasks (think of them as micro-quests). Don't skip these—they're where the real XP lives.

3. **Customize Your Game Plan:** Not every strategy will work for every player. Take what resonates, adapt the rest, and build a system that suits your personal playstyle.

4. **Track Your Progress:** Keep a notebook or digital tracker handy to record your goals, wins, and insights as you move through the book. Think of it as your in-game journal.

5. **Have Fun Along the Way:** Life's grind doesn't have to be boring. This book is designed to make personal growth feel as engaging and rewarding as a well-designed game.

The only rule? Keep playing. Whether you hit setbacks, discover unexpected power-ups, or decide to pause and restart, remember that every move you make is part of the game. Ready? Press Start and let's begin!

About Us

Hi there, I'm Ken Konet, M.Ed., MBA, an Instructional Designer by day and an unapologetic gamer by night. For over two decades, I've designed learning systems for Fortune 500 companies, watching grown adults light up when training stops feeling like homework and starts feeling like play. That moment—when someone realizes they're having fun while developing genuine skills—never gets old.

But I didn't write this book alone. My co-author Ibrahim Roble is a writer, technologist, and creative strategist who brings an analytical edge to everything we build together. And my wife Isabella "Izzy" Green—professional handywoman by day, elite gamer by night—is the one who taught me that video games aren't just button-mashing. She's my co-op partner, my gaming coach, and the secret weapon behind this book's credibility.

The three of us regularly team up for epic multiplayer sessions, trading blows with virtual bosses and occasionally yelling, "Why did you aggro the whole dungeon?!" We also love gathering around the table with friends for board games, card games, and the occasional DnD dice roll that decides our fate. And we don't just play face-to-face—we play games with friends online via webcam, showcasing our boards, cards, and questionable strategies. Technology today makes it easy and fun to play games with anyone, anywhere.

Why did we write this book? Because we believe that gaming is more than just entertainment. It's a framework for growth, a way to stay motivated, and a toolkit for conquering life's challenges. Whether it's tackling daily quests, grinding for achievements, or forming alliances with fellow players, the lessons we learn in games are directly transferable to real life. So if you're ready to stop playing passively and start living like the hero of your own story, let's hit the start button together. Welcome to *Gamify Your Life for Success*—it's going to be a wild, rewarding ride.

Introduction

Welcome, hero. You've just pressed "Start" on the ultimate quest—a journey to gamify your life and unlock your full potential. This isn't your typical self-help book, filled with flowery platitudes or vague promises about "living your best life." No, this is more like the manual that comes with a killer RPG—full of cheat codes, strategies, and enough sarcastic commentary to keep you entertained as you level up.

So why are you here? Maybe you feel stuck in a grind, endlessly farming resources with no sense of progress. Maybe life feels like a game on Nightmare difficulty, and you're wielding a rusty dagger against an endgame boss. Or maybe, just maybe, you're tired of playing a passive role and ready to take control of your own story.

Whatever brought you here, I'm glad you made it. Now, grab your controller (or dice, or cards), and let's dive into how gamification can turn even the most mundane parts of life into an epic adventure.

Imagine life as a video game—a vast open-world RPG (role-playing game) where you're both the protagonist and the programmer. You've got the controller, a blank character sheet, and the ultimate cheat code: the ability to rewrite the rules of the game to work in your favor. Sounds thrilling, right? But here's the catch: most people are playing this game of life on "impossible" mode without even realizing it. Worse still, they're stuck grinding for experience points (XP) in all the wrong dungeons, battling mini-bosses that aren't worth the loot, and ignoring the treasure chests hidden in plain sight.

Now, let me ask you this: how would life change if you treated it as the greatest game you've ever played? What if you could leverage the same skills you've honed in games—strategic thinking, resource management, grinding with purpose—to create a life so productive and fulfilling that even your past self would be jealous? Spoiler alert: You can!

But before we dive headfirst into rewriting your life's code, let's address the elephant in the room. Why the heck does adulting suck so much?

Why Gamify Your Life?

First, let's address the question every skeptic is asking: "Why should I gamify my life?"

The answer is simple—because it works. Gamification taps into the same psychological principles that make games so addictive. Dopamine loops, instant feedback, clear goals, and a sense of progress are all baked into gaming. In life, these same principles can help you stay motivated, overcome obstacles, and, most importantly, have fun while you're doing it.

Think about it: games are structured to keep you engaged. They give you a clear mission ("Save the princess!"), measurable progress ("You've leveled up!"), and rewards that make the grind worthwhile ("Here's a shiny new sword!"). Life, on the other hand, often feels like an unpatched beta—messy, directionless, and full of random encounters with no clear rewards.

But what if you could change that? What if you could take the mechanics that make games so compelling and apply them to your own goals, habits, and challenges? That's what this book is all about.

Life is a Game

Life isn't just an open-world RPG—it's a mashup of every game genre you've ever played. Sometimes it's a tactical board game where every move counts, like *Chess* or *Risk*. Other times, it's a card game like *Poker* where you're making the best of the hand you've been dealt. And then there are the moments where life feels like a dice roll in *Dungeons & Dragons*—a mix of strategy, luck, and sheer determination to roll that nat 20 when it matters most.

The beauty of this book is that it's not just about video games. No matter what kind of player you are—card shark, dice slinger, board game strategist, or joystick warrior—you'll find tools here to help you design your best game plan

Life as the Ultimate Open-World RPG

Let's frame this in gamer terms. Imagine your life as an open-world RPG. You're the main character—complete with strengths, weaknesses, and a backstory that may or may not include a tragic orphan origin. The world around you is your sandbox, filled with quests, NPCs, and the occasional random event that derails your plans (hello, flat tire).

The problem is that most of us aren't playing the game to its fullest potential. We're wandering aimlessly, skipping the main questline, and wondering why we're still stuck at Level 1. Worse, some of us are playing on autopilot, letting the game play us instead of the other way around.

Here's the good news: you have the power to change that. By gamifying your life, you can take control of the narrative, set your own goals, and turn even the most mundane tasks into exciting quests. Want to get in shape? That's a fitness grind. Need to ace a work project? That's a boss battle. Trying to learn a new skill? Welcome to your skill tree.

The Hero's Journey: Your First Quest

Every great story starts with a hero's journey. Think Frodo with the One Ring, Link with his Master Sword, or Mario on his eternal quest to rescue Peach. Your journey begins here, with this book as your guide.

Like any good RPG, you'll face challenges along the way. There will be grindy parts, frustrating moments, and the occasional setback that feels like a total wipe. But there will also be victories, power-ups, and those magical moments where everything just clicks, and you realize you're leveling up in ways you never imagined.

And don't worry—you won't be doing this alone. This book is packed with tools, strategies, and exercises to help you every step of the way. Think of me as your friendly neighborhood quest giver, here to nudge you in the right direction and occasionally crack a sarcastic joke when you need it most.

Welcome to the Tutorial Level

Adulting sucks for one simple reason: the game is rigged against you. It's like starting a new RPG and realizing your character was nerfed from the start—low stats, no gear, and no clear quest log. From the moment you hit Level 18 (or thereabouts), society hands you a controller and says, "Figure it out." No manual. No tutorial. Just an endless grind of bills, jobs, taxes, and an existential dread that comes standard with every adulthood DLC (Dead Life Choices, for the uninitiated).

But here's the thing: the game doesn't have to stay rigged. Unlike that one infuriating level in *Dark Souls* where everything wants you dead, life can be hacked. You just need to learn the mechanics—and that's where this book comes in. Think of this as your ultimate strategy guide, complete with tips to buff your stats, avoid unnecessary de-buffs, and tackle life's toughest bosses.

We're not here to survive the grind; we're here to dominate it. Together, we're going to take the principles of gamification—the art of making mundane things fun—and turn your life into the most engaging, rewarding, and downright entertaining game you've ever played.

But First, a Reality Check

Gamification isn't some woo-woo self-help gimmick. It's science, grounded in psychology and neuroscience. It's what keeps you glued to games like *The Legend of Zelda* or *Stardew Valley,* where every quest, no matter how small, feels meaningful. It's the dopamine rush you get from leveling up, the satisfaction of clearing your quest log, and the thrill of unlocking that rare achievement you didn't think was possible.

Here's the kicker: the same principles that make video games addictive can make real life fulfilling. The key lies in reprogramming your brain to treat your daily grind like an epic quest.

Take it from me—gamification works. As an instructional designer, I've spent over a decade using these principles to engage learners, boost motivation, and transform the dullest corporate trainings into experiences people actually enjoy. If gamification can make compliance training bearable, imagine what it can do for your life.

The Core Mechanics: How Gamification Works

Before we dive into the nitty-gritty, let's talk about the core mechanics of gamification. These are the elements that make games so engaging—and, spoiler alert, they work just as well in real life.

1. **Clear Goals:** Every good game gives you a clear objective. Whether it's defeating a final boss or collecting 100 coins, you know exactly what you're working toward. In life, setting clear goals gives you direction and purpose.
2. **Progress Tracking:** Games constantly show you how far you've come, whether it's through XP bars, achievements, or leaderboards. In life, tracking your progress helps you stay motivated and see the impact of your efforts.
3. **Rewards:** From shiny loot to rare cards, rewards keep you engaged and excited. In life, creating meaningful rewards for your achievements can make even the toughest grind feel worthwhile.
4. **Feedback Loops:** Games provide instant feedback—whether you're winning, losing, or just messing up royally. In life, feedback (both from yourself and others) helps you learn, adapt, and grow.
5. **Challenge and Mastery:** The best games hit that sweet spot between too easy and too hard, keeping you in a state of flow. In life, finding challenges that push you without overwhelming you is the key to sustained growth.

What This Book Will Teach You

Here's what you'll gain from reading *Gamify Your Life for Success*:

- How to break down your goals into manageable quests that keep you motivated.
- Strategies for building habits through daily challenges and tracking your progress.
- Tools to tackle life's obstacles and boss battles with confidence and resilience.
- Techniques for forming alliances, building a support network, and leveling up as a team.
- Insights into lifelong learning and how to keep growing even after you've "beaten the game."

This isn't a one-size-fits-all guide. It's a flexible system that you can adapt to fit your playstyle, whether you're a completionist who wants to tackle every side quest or a casual player who just wants to enjoy the ride.

The Roadmap Ahead

Think of this book as your strategy guide. By the time you finish, you'll know how to:

- **Design Your Own Game:** Define your core mission, build your character, and set your quest log.
- **Level Up Like a Pro:** Develop habits and skills that make progress feel effortless.
- **Overcome Boss Battles:** Learn how to tackle life's toughest challenges without rage-quitting.
- **Form Your Party:** Build a network of allies who make the journey more rewarding.
- **Unlock Expansion Packs:** Adapt to new levels of success and keep the game exciting.

But before we jump into the mechanics, there's one crucial rule you need to embrace: **this is your game.** Your goals, your values, and your idea of success are the only metrics that matter. Forget about society's "win conditions." If your idea of winning is becoming the ultimate sourdough baker or finally keeping a houseplant alive, then that's your endgame.

Level 1: Rewriting the Rules

So, how do we start? By rewriting the rules. That's what Part A of this introduction is all about—helping you unlearn the bad programming you've picked up and showing you that life is more malleable than you think. You don't need to play by society's broken rules. You can create your own win conditions and choose your difficulty level.

But beware, because this isn't a cheat code—it's a mindset shift. A real-life patch update that requires you to stop playing the victim and start acting like the hero. Sound intimidating? Don't worry. Heroes aren't born; they're made, one side quest at a time. Each side quest adds XP, loot, or a rare skill point. It's all about grinding smarter, not harder.

Ready to dive into the second half of this introduction? Good, because in **Part B**, we'll take a closer look at why games are so addictive and how to harness that same magic in your everyday life. Spoiler alert: it's all about feedback, rewards, and a dash of creativity.

Why Games Are So Addictive (and How to Use That to Your Advantage)

Let's start with a confession: games are designed to hook you. Every level, every achievement, every perfectly timed loot drop—it's all part of a grand scheme to keep you coming back for more. But unlike that endless scroll of doom on social media, games offer something far more rewarding: a sense of progress, purpose, and mastery.

So, what makes games so irresistible? It all boils down to three key elements: **feedback, rewards, and challenge.** These are the holy trinity of engagement, and if you can learn to weave them into your daily life, you'll find yourself waking up excited to tackle even the most mundane tasks.

The Feedback Loop: Your Built-In Motivation Engine

Ever notice how games constantly tell you how you're doing? You earn XP for completing quests, see progress bars filling up, and get immediate feedback when you succeed (or fail). This feedback loop keeps you engaged because it creates a direct connection between your actions and your outcomes.

In real life, feedback is often slower and more ambiguous. You spend months working on a project, only to hear, "Good job," or worse, nothing at all. That's like finishing a 50-hour RPG only to be told, "Game over, I guess." No wonder real life feels like a grind!

Here's how we fix that:

- **Create Your Own Feedback Loop.** Think of this as your personal HUD (heads-up display)—a real-time tracker that shows you whether you're gaining XP or accidentally taking a de-buff to your energy bar. Break your goals into smaller tasks and track your progress visually. Use apps, journals, or even sticky notes to give yourself instant updates on how far you've come.

- **Celebrate Every Win.** Even if it's something as small as finishing an email, give yourself a mental high-five. Games reward you for tiny victories, and your brain craves that recognition.

Remember, feedback isn't just about measuring progress; it's about reinforcing the idea that your efforts matter. When you can see the impact of what you're doing, even the most repetitive tasks start to feel meaningful.

Rewards: The Sweet Taste of Victory

Why do we spend hours grinding for a legendary sword or completing 100% of a game's achievements? Because the rewards make it worth it. Whether it's a shiny new item, a rare badge, or just the satisfaction of checking something off a list, rewards give us a reason to keep going.

In life, rewards are just as crucial—but often neglected. We're so focused on big goals (like buying a house or landing a dream job) that we forget to reward ourselves for the smaller wins along the way. This is a mistake because, without regular rewards, motivation fizzles out faster than a discount health potion.

Here's how to gamify your rewards:

- **Set Mini-Boss Milestones.** Every milestone is a loot chest. The more you grind through these mini-bosses, the more you'll unlock buffs for motivation and confidence. Break big goals into smaller checkpoints, and reward yourself for reaching them. Finished a tough workout? Treat yourself to your favorite playlist. Crushed a deadline? Celebrate with a guilt-free Netflix binge.
- **Choose Rewards That Matter.** Make sure your rewards align with your values and goals. If you're trying to save money, don't splurge on a shopping spree—find a reward that feels indulgent but still supports your mission.

When you start associating effort with positive outcomes, you'll train your brain to crave progress. Suddenly, grinding through your to-do list won't feel like a chore; it'll feel like a quest with epic loot waiting at the end. It's like fragging weaker mobs in a dungeon before taking on the raid boss. Every step gets you closer to the win.

The Goldilocks Rule of Challenge: Not Too Hard, Not Too Easy

The final piece of the puzzle is challenge. Games are addictive because they strike the perfect balance between frustration and boredom. If a game is too easy, you'll quit out of sheer disinterest. Too hard, and you'll rage-quit before you even reach the tutorial boss. And we've all been there—facing a boss fight under-leveled with no potions in our inventory. It's brutal, but preparation and leveling up make all the difference.

Life works the same way. If your goals are too ambitious, you'll feel overwhelmed and give up. If they're too simple, you'll lose interest and procrastinate. The key is to find your "Goldilocks Zone" where tasks are challenging enough to keep you engaged but achievable enough to give you a sense of accomplishment.

Here's how to apply the Goldilocks Rule:

- **Adjust the Difficulty.** If a task feels impossible, break it into smaller steps. If it's too easy, add a layer of complexity to keep things interesting.
- **Embrace Flow State.** Flow happens when you're so immersed in an activity that you lose track of time. To achieve this, pick tasks that align with your skills and push you just enough to stay focused without feeling overwhelmed.

Life doesn't have to be a grind. By balancing challenge with your skill level, you'll find yourself enjoying the process as much as the results.

A Note on Failure: It's Part of the Game

Let me say this upfront: you're going to fail. A lot. And that's okay. Failure is a core mechanic in life, just like it is in games. Every "Game Over" screen is just a chance to respawn, learn from your mistakes, and try again.

Think of failure as XP in disguise. Every misstep teaches you something, and every retry brings you closer to success. The only way to truly fail is to stop playing.

Ready to Press Start?

When you combine feedback, rewards, and challenge, you create a system that keeps you engaged, motivated, and happy. This is the secret sauce that makes games so addictive—and it's the same formula we'll use to gamify your life. It's like building the ultimate build—stacking buffs, avoiding unnecessary nerfs, and optimizing your playstyle for maximum fun and success.

Think of this chapter as your tutorial level. Now that you understand the mechanics, it's time to start designing your own game. In the next chapter, we'll dive into creating your character, defining your mission, and setting up your first quest log.

You're about to take control of the greatest game you'll ever play. So grab your metaphorical controller, hit "Start," and get ready to level up like never before.

This is your story, your game, your adventure. The quests are yours to create, the skills are yours to master, and the victories are yours to claim.

So what are you waiting for? Pick up your controller, shuffle your deck, or roll the dice. It's time to press start and gamify your life for success.

Let's do this.

Chapter 1: Choose Your Character

Welcome to character creation, the most crucial part of any RPG. You've just loaded up a brand-new game called *Life*, and congratulations—you're already stuck with a character build you didn't choose. No rerolls. No customization. Just a randomly generated bundle of stats, traits, and flaws that you didn't ask for. Oh, and spoiler alert: this isn't *The Sims*. You can't just hit Ctrl+Shift+C and type "motherlode" for unlimited cash.

But don't worry, because while your starting build might feel like a de-buff nightmare, this chapter is all about figuring out what makes your character tick. Think of this as the "skills and talents" menu in your life game. We're going to hack into your stats, discover your hidden buffs, and start tweaking your build so you can frag the competition (or, at least, stop rage-quitting every Monday).

Step 1: Know Your Base Stats

In every RPG, your base stats determine how you play the game. Are you a tank with max strength and zero charisma? A rogue with high agility but paper-thin health points? Or maybe you're a bard—a little bit of everything, but mostly just here to entertain yourself and maybe annoy your friends.

Here's the thing: your base stats don't define you, but they do set the stage for how you'll level up. You might not be able to change your starting numbers, but you *can* stack buffs to turn weaknesses into strengths.

For example, let's say your charisma stat is so low that talking to your neighbors feels like a boss fight. That doesn't mean you're doomed to awkward silences and solo raids forever. It just means you need to find ways to compensate. Maybe that's equipping the "self-deprecating humor" buff or grinding in the "small talk" dungeon until your conversational skills are strong enough to survive a networking event.

Pro Tip: Stop comparing your stats to everyone else's. Some people are born with OP (overpowered) builds. Good for them. You're here to optimize your *own* character, not cry about someone else's legendary gear.

Step 2: Identify Your Character Class

Choosing your class is the ultimate game-changer. It's the difference between being a healer who keeps everyone alive and a DPS (damage per second) main who solos everything until they inevitably wipe in a dungeon because they didn't bring any potions.

In real life, your class is less about what you do and more about how you approach challenges. Are you the strategist who plans every move, the tank who absorbs hits for the team, or the wildcard who just wings it and hopes for a crit? Here's how to figure it out:

1. **What Role Do You Naturally Gravitate Toward?**
   Think about group projects. (Yes, I know, PTSD.) Are you the one organizing the chaos, doing all the work, or just there for moral support? This gives you a clue about your natural class.

2. **What Skills Do You Enjoy Using?**
   Are you a numbers nerd, a creative powerhouse, or the ultimate people person? Your skills should align with your class—because nothing's worse than being a bard who hates performing.

3. **What Challenges Do You Love Crushing?**
   Maybe you're a healer who thrives on helping others, or a rogue who lives for sneaky side quests. Your favorite challenges reveal your ideal playstyle.

Pro Tip: Don't pigeonhole yourself. Real life isn't a game where you're locked into one class forever. You can respec(redistribute your skill points) anytime you want. Just don't forget to save your progress.

Step 3: Equip Your Starter Gear

You wouldn't charge into a boss fight wearing beginner armor and wielding a wooden sword, right? (Unless you're doing some weird speedrun challenge—no judgment.) The same goes for real life. Before you tackle big quests, you need to gear up.

Starter gear isn't flashy, but it gets the job done. It's the metaphorical equivalent of a basic LinkedIn profile, a decent pair of shoes, and an alarm clock that wakes you up. Sure, it's not a legendary artifact, but every hero starts somewhere.

Here's what your starter gear might look like IRL:

- **Your Weapon:** This is your primary skill or talent—the thing you're naturally good at. Maybe it's writing, coding, or making the world's best memes.
- **Your Armor:** These are your defenses—habits and routines that protect your energy and keep you in the game. Think meal prepping, regular exercise, or saying "no" to unnecessary drama.
- **Your Trinkets:** The little extras that give you a boost. This could be a motivational podcast, a killer playlist, or even your favorite coffee mug that somehow makes mornings less terrible.

Pro Tip: Don't underestimate the power of upgrades. Your starter gear might be basic, but with time and effort, it'll evolve into something legendary.

Step 4: Beware of Early-Game Traps

Every game has traps—those sneaky little pitfalls designed to make you question your life choices. In real life, these traps take the form of bad habits, toxic people, and distractions that drain your XP without offering any rewards.

Here are some common traps to watch out for:

- **The "Comparison" Trap:** You're busy grinding, but it feels like everyone else is already max level. Ignore it. They might just have a good PR campaign.
- **The "All-Or-Nothing" Trap:** If you can't do something perfectly, you don't do it at all. Newsflash: even half-finished quests give XP.
- **The "Procrastination" Trap:** You tell yourself you'll tackle the big boss tomorrow. **Reality Check**: tomorrow never comes.

Pro Tip: Traps are inevitable, but they're also avoidable if you stay alert. Treat them like mini-bosses—annoying but beatable with the right strategy.

Bio Break: AFK for a Minute!

By now, you should have a solid understanding of your character's base stats, class, and starter gear. But remember, this is just the beginning. Every great hero starts as a noob. The key is to keep leveling up, one quest at a time.

So, you've got your base stats, picked a character class, and geared up for the grind. Congratulations! You've officially made it through the tutorial. But before you start fragging through life like it's *Call of Duty,* let's tackle the big question: what's your mission?

Because here's the thing—no matter how good your stats are or how epic your gear looks, wandering around aimlessly will get you nowhere. It's like playing *Skyrim* and spending 400 hours picking flowers and hoarding cheese wheels instead of slaying dragons. Fun? Maybe. Fulfilling? Definitely not.

This is where your **Main Quest** comes in. It's the driving force behind your game, the thing that keeps you leveling up, even when life throws curveballs (or, you know, RNGesus decides to ruin your day).

Step 1: Define Your Main Quest

Your Main Quest is your big-picture goal, your reason for playing the game of life in the first place. It doesn't have to be world-changing (though if you want to be the next Tony Stark, go for it). It just has to matter to *you.*

Think of it like this: if your life were an RPG, what would the final boss look like? Is it financial freedom, starting a business, writing a novel, or finally figuring out how to keep a houseplant alive? Whatever it is, that's your endgame.

Pro Tip: Don't overthink it. Your Main Quest doesn't need to be set in stone. Think of it as a flexible objective—like when a game updates its DLC, and suddenly the stakes get higher.

Step 2: Break It Into Side Quests

Every gamer knows that the Main Quest can feel overwhelming if you don't break it into smaller steps. That's where Side Quests come in. These are the manageable chunks of progress that get you closer to the endgame without making you want to rage-quit.

Here's how to create your Side Quests:

1. **Start with Milestones:** Break your Main Quest into key checkpoints. For example, if your goal is to run a marathon, your milestones might include running a 5K, a 10K, and eventually a half marathon.
2. **Add Sub-Quests:** These are the smaller tasks that support your milestones. For the marathon example, a sub-quest might be creating a training plan or investing in good running shoes (because no one wants to fight the "blisters" mini-boss).
3. **Include Optional Quests:** These are the fun extras that aren't necessary but add value. Think of them as the "collect all the Korok seeds" of your life—rewarding, but not essential.

Pro Tip: Side Quests aren't just about productivity. They're also about making the journey enjoyable. Add some quests that are purely for fun—like learning a new hobby or discovering the best taco joint in town.

Step 3: Build Your Quest Log

Once you've mapped out your Main Quest and Side Quests, it's time to organize them in a way that keeps you on track. This is where your Quest Log comes in. Think of it as your personal roadmap, complete with objectives, deadlines, and rewards.

Here's what your Quest Log might include:

- **Quest Name:** A brief, catchy title for each quest (e.g., "Operation Fit AF" or "Project Pay Off Student Loans Without Crying").
- **Objective:** What you need to accomplish. Be specific—vague quests lead to vague results.
- **Deadline:** A realistic timeline for completing the quest.
- **Reward:** What you'll get when you complete the quest (because no one grinds for free).

Pro Tip: Use tools like apps, spreadsheets, or even an old-school notebook to track your progress. Bonus points if you make it visually appealing—think stickers, color-coding, or digital badges.

Step 4: Watch Out for Quest Fatigue

Here's the thing about quests: it's easy to get overwhelmed when you're juggling too many at once. In gaming terms, this is called "quest fatigue," and it's a real de-buff to your productivity.

To avoid burning out, follow these rules:

1. **Limit Active Quests:** Focus on 3–5 quests at a time. Any more, and you risk spreading yourself too thin.
2. **Prioritize Your Objectives:** Some quests are time-sensitive, while others can wait. Tackle the high-priority ones first, and save the rest for later.

3. **Don't Skip Rest Points:** Even the most epic heroes need to recharge. Build downtime into your schedule to avoid hitting zero stamina.

Pro Tip: If you're feeling stuck, revisit your Quest Log and see if any objectives need tweaking. Sometimes a small adjustment—like lowering the difficulty level—can make all the difference.

Step 5: Embrace Random Encounters

No game is complete without random encounters—the unplanned events that throw you off course but often lead to unexpected rewards. In real life, these might be surprise opportunities, chance meetings, or even failures that teach you something valuable.

Here's how to handle them like a pro:

- **Stay Open-Minded:** Not every random encounter is a trap. Some might lead to side quests you didn't even know you wanted.
- **Adapt Quickly:** Treat unexpected challenges as opportunities to flex your problem-solving skills.
- **Keep Your XP in Perspective:** Even if an encounter doesn't go your way, it still adds to your experience points.

Pro Tip: Random encounters are where some of the best stories come from. Don't shy away from them just because they weren't in your original plan.

The Power of Gamification

The principles of gamification aren't exclusive to video games. Think about deck-building games like *Dominion* or *Magic: The Gathering*. Every card you add to your deck feels like progress—just like every skill or habit you build in life. Or consider cooperative board games like *Pandemic*, where you and your team must adapt to challenges together. These games engage players because they're structured around clear goals, meaningful decisions, and rewards for strategic thinking.

In your life, gamification is about designing a system that works the same way: a structure that keeps you engaged, motivated, and always moving forward, one 'turn' at a time

Ready Player One (That's You)

Now that you've defined your character, chosen your class, and mapped out your quest log, you're officially ready to start playing. Remember, the key to success isn't just grinding—it's grinding with purpose. Every side quest, every random encounter, every hard-fought victory adds to your story.

And if you're still feeling a little unprepared, don't worry. Every great game starts with a learning curve. The important thing is that you've hit "Start" and are ready to play. In the next chapter, we'll tackle the art of leveling up—because no one wants to stay a Level 1 noob forever. Let's buff those stats and turn you into the hero you were meant to be.

Chapter 2: Level Up Your Stats

So, you've chosen your character, equipped your starter gear, and scribbled your Main Quest into your shiny new Quest Log. You're officially ready to start playing. But here's the thing— You didn't pick up the controller to spend your entire life in the tutorial zone. Sure, Level 1 is great for learning the ropes, but you'll need to level up those stats if you want to start taking on bigger challenges (and, let's be honest, looking cooler doing it).

Think of leveling up as the ultimate buff. Every point you gain makes you faster, stronger, smarter, or just a little less likely to wipe during your next boss battle. But before you start grinding, you need to know *what* to level up—and more importantly, how.

Part A

Step 1: Analyze Your Current Stats

Before you can start allocating skill points, you need to figure out where you stand. Are you a high-intelligence, low-strength scholar? A charisma-heavy, agility-light social butterfly? Or maybe you're a jack-of-all-trades, master of none (don't worry, we'll fix that).

Here's how to analyze your stats in real life:

1. **Identify Your Strengths:** What are you already good at? These are your high stats—the ones that give you a natural advantage in certain areas.
2. **Spot Your Weaknesses:** Which areas feel like a constant struggle? These are your low stats, also known as your personal de-buffs.
3. **Find the Gaps:** Are there skills you've never invested in but wish you had? These are the stats you'll want to start leveling up.

Pro Tip: Be honest with yourself. Pretending you're good at everything doesn't make you a hero; it makes you a liability. A balanced build starts with self-awareness.

Step 2: Choose Your Focus Stats

Every great hero knows you can't level up everything at once. If you try to spread your skill points too thin, you'll end up as the RPG equivalent of a tofu sword—technically functional, but not very effective. Instead, focus on the stats that will have the biggest impact on your Main Quest.

Here are some common focus stats to consider:

- **Strength:** Perfect for physical goals like improving fitness or tackling home improvement projects.
- **Intelligence:** Ideal for learning new skills, solving problems, or crushing trivia night at the local bar.
- **Charisma:** The go-to stat for building relationships, networking, and winning people over with your charm.
- **Agility:** Great for improving flexibility, speed, or just making sure you don't trip over your own feet.
- **Endurance:** A must-have for anyone dealing with long-term projects, marathon training, or the sheer grind of adulting.

Pro Tip: Focus on one or two primary stats and one secondary stat. Think of it like building a DPS main with a bit of healing on the side—specialization is key, but versatility never hurts.

Step 3: Grind with Purpose

Let's be real—leveling up in real life isn't as simple as farming XP in a low-level dungeon. There's no endless stream of goblins to frag, and most of your "loot" is just stuff you already paid for. But here's the good news: real-life grinding is *way* more rewarding when you do it with purpose.

Here's how to make your grind more effective:

1. **Set Clear Goals:** Grinding without a goal is like wandering into an open-world game with no quest markers. Decide what you want to achieve and why it matters.

2. **Track Your Progress:** Use tools like apps, journals, or spreadsheets to keep tabs on your XP gains. Watching those numbers climb is a reward in itself.

3. **Celebrate Milestones:** Every level-up deserves a mini celebration. Treat yourself to something small but meaningful—like upgrading your "coffee potion" to the fancy café version.

Pro Tip: Avoid grinding in the wrong areas. If your goal is to improve your agility, don't waste time stacking strength. Stay focused on the stats that matter most.

Step 4: Equip Passive Buffs

In gaming, passive buffs are the low-maintenance perks that make life easier without requiring constant effort. In real life, these are your habits and routines—the things you do automatically that boost your stats over time.

Here are some examples of passive buffs you can equip:

- **Morning Routine Buff:** Start your day with a ritual that energizes you, like stretching, meditating, or chugging a health potion (a.k.a. water).

- **Time Management Buff:** Use tools like calendars or to-do lists to keep your schedule on track.

- **Energy Buff:** Prioritize sleep, nutrition, and exercise to keep your stamina bar full.

Pro Tip: Don't underestimate the power of small changes. A tiny buff might not seem like much, but over time, it can make a huge difference.

Step 5: Beware of Stat Nerfs

Just like some games love to nerf your favorite character, real life has a way of nerfing your stats if you're not careful. Stress, bad habits, and burnout can all chip away at your progress, leaving you feeling like a low-level scrub.

Here's how to avoid unnecessary nerfs:

1. **Manage Stress:** Find healthy ways to cope with stress, like exercise, journaling, or yelling into a pillow.
2. **Avoid Toxic Influences:** Cut ties with people, environments, or habits that drain your energy or confidence.
3. **Take Breaks:** Even the most dedicated players need to log off sometimes. Rest isn't a waste of time—it's how you recharge your mana.

Pro Tip: If you do get nerfed, don't panic. Every hero takes a hit now and then. The key is to bounce back stronger than before.

Leveling Up is a Lifelong Grind

Here's the reality: leveling up your stats isn't a one-and-done deal. It's a continuous process—a never-ending grind that gets a little easier (and a lot more fun) with time. The good news? Every small gain adds up, and before you know it, you'll be taking on challenges that once felt impossible.

In **Part B**, we'll dive into the art of building synergy between your stats and unlocking special abilities that take your game to the next level. Because let's face it—what's the point of leveling up if you're not going to unlock some epic skills along the way?

Bio Break: AFK for a Minute!

Now that you've learned the basics of leveling up your stats, let's kick it up a notch. Because what's the point of grinding for XP if you're not unlocking some epic abilities and becoming the absolute beast you were born to be? Part B is all about synergy—making your stats work together like a perfectly balanced raid team—and unlocking those special abilities that make life more fun, productive, and rewarding.

Step 6: Synergy – When Stats Work Together

In gaming, synergy is what happens when your team's abilities complement each other to create something unstoppable. In real life, it's the same principle: when your strengths and skills align, you can handle almost anything.

Let's break it down with a few examples:

1. **Strength + Endurance:** Want to run a marathon or crush your fitness goals? Strength gives you power, while endurance keeps you going. Together, they're the ultimate combo for physical challenges.
2. **Charisma + Intelligence:** Ever notice how the smartest person in the room doesn't always get ahead? That's because charisma amplifies intelligence, making your ideas more persuasive and your connections stronger.
3. **Agility + Strength:** Whether you're tackling parkour (in real life or in *Assassin's Creed*) or just trying not to fall flat on your face at the gym, this combo is all about balance and power.

Pro Tip: Think of synergy as your personal meta build. Focus on pairing stats that naturally complement each other, and watch how your efficiency skyrockets.

Step 7: Unlock Your Special Abilities

Leveling up isn't just about stats—it's also about unlocking those game-changing abilities that make you feel like a total badass. In life, these abilities are your advanced skills, habits, and mindsets that take you from good to legendary.

Here's how to identify and unlock your special abilities:

1. **Look for Patterns:** What do you excel at without even trying? These natural talents are often the foundation of your most powerful abilities.
2. **Experiment with Skill Trees:** Just like in games, your abilities in life often branch out into new areas. For example, if you're great at public speaking, you might unlock leadership or teaching as secondary skills.
3. **Invest in Mastery:** Unlocking an ability is only the beginning. Mastery comes from practice, repetition, and a willingness to fail spectacularly before you get it right.

Pro Tip: Don't sleep on "soft skills." Things like communication, adaptability, and time management might not sound flashy, but they're the kind of abilities that make everything else easier.

Step 8: Manage Your Cooldowns

In gaming, cooldowns are the time it takes for an ability to recharge after you use it. In life, it's the same idea—your energy, focus, and creativity need time to recover. If you don't manage your cooldowns, you'll end up spamming abilities until you burn out.

Here's how to manage your cooldowns effectively:

1. **Pay Attention to Energy Levels:** Are you a morning person or a night owl? Align your most challenging tasks with your peak energy times.
2. **Schedule Breaks:** Build recovery time into your daily routine, whether that's a short walk, a power nap, or a quick gaming session to recharge.
3. **Avoid Overuse:** Just because you *can* work nonstop doesn't mean you should. Pace yourself to avoid nerfing your stamina.

Pro Tip: Think of recovery as part of the grind. Just like upgrading your gear, recharging your energy is an investment in long-term success.

Step 9: Level Up Your Allies

Every great hero needs a party, and in life, that means surrounding yourself with people who inspire, challenge, and support you. But here's the kicker: your allies are only as strong as the effort you put into leveling them up.

Here's how to build a strong party:

1. **Recruit the Right People:** Look for allies who complement your stats. If you're a high-charisma rogue, find a tank who can take hits for you. If you're a strength-based fighter, recruit someone with intelligence or agility.
2. **Invest in Relationships:** Just like in games, relationships require time and effort to grow. Show up, stay connected, and support your allies in their own quests.
3. **Share Buffs:** When you succeed, lift others up with you. A strong party benefits everyone.

Pro Tip: Beware of party members who bring de-buffs instead of boosts. If someone consistently drains your energy, it might be time to swap them out for a better fit.

Step 10: Embrace the Endgame Mindset

Here's the truth: leveling up isn't just about grinding for XP. It's about building a mindset that keeps you motivated, resilient, and ready for whatever the game throws at you. This is the endgame mindset—the mental framework that turns setbacks into challenges, challenges into progress, and progress into victory.

Here's how to embrace the endgame mindset:

1. **Focus on Growth:** The goal isn't to be perfect; it's to be better than you were yesterday. Every failure, every struggle, every hard-fought win adds to your experience points.
2. **Keep Adapting:** Life is like a constantly updating game. New challenges, new bosses, new loot—staying flexible is the key to staying ahead.

3. **Celebrate the Grind:** Remember, the grind is where the magic happens. Those tiny, incremental gains might not feel like much now, but they add up to something epic over time.

Pro Tip: The endgame isn't about finishing the game; it's about loving the process. When you treat every day as an opportunity to grow, leveling up stops feeling like a chore and starts feeling like an adventure.

Your Hero's Journey Continues

Congratulations, you've officially leveled up your understanding of stats, synergy, and special abilities. But this is just the beginning. Every new level brings new challenges, and every new challenge is a chance to prove your mettle.

In the next chapter, we'll tackle one of the most important mechanics in life's game: building habits that stick. Because no hero ever saved the world without a solid routine (and maybe a little help from their party). Get ready to buff your discipline, nerf your bad habits, and unlock the ultimate cheat code for success: consistency.

Chapter 3: Building Habits Through Daily Quests

Welcome to the guild, Initiate! You've got your character sorted, stats leveled up, and a shiny Quest Log full of big dreams and smaller steps. Now we're going to tackle the true endgame mechanic of life: habits. Think of habits as your passive buffs—once you set them up, they do the work for you in the background. No cooldowns, no micro-transactions, just pure efficiency.

The problem? Building habits is about as fun as grinding for XP in the most boring dungeon ever. But that's why we're here. By the time you finish this chapter, you'll know how to turn boring habit-building into a series of satisfying daily quests—complete with rewards, progress tracking, and the occasional achievement unlock.

Step 1: Understand the Power of Streaks and Combos

Let's start with the basics. In gaming, streaks and combos are the holy grail of efficiency. Whether it's pulling off a killer combo in *Street Fighter* or racking up headshots in *Call of Duty*, chaining actions together makes everything more powerful. Habits work the same way.

When you repeat an action daily, you're building a streak. The longer the streak, the more momentum you gain. Miss a day, and you're back to Level 1. It's brutal but fair—just like Dark Souls.

Here's how to build your streaks:

1. **Start Small:** Your first daily quest should be something so easy it's almost laughable. Drink one glass of water. Do one push-up. Draw one card for your creative writing deck.
2. **Stack Your Actions:** Once you've got one habit rolling, stack another one onto it. This is called "habit stacking,"

but let's call it a combo move because that sounds cooler. Example: You brush your teeth (the setup), and then you floss (the finisher). Boom—combo completed.

3. **Track Your Streaks:** Use a calendar, app, or even a whiteboard to mark every day you complete your quest. Watching that streak grow is as satisfying as watching your XP bar fill up.

Pro Tip: Treat streaks like your K/D ratio (kill/death ratio, for the uninitiated). You want to keep it high, not because anyone's judging you, but because you know deep down you're better than a broken streak.

Step 2: Choose Your Daily Quests Wisely

Not all quests are created equal. Some are worth the grind, while others are better left to NPCs (non-playable characters). Your job is to figure out which habits will give you the biggest buffs to your stats and overall gameplay.

The Perfect Daily Quest Checklist:

- **It's Relevant:** Does this habit help you progress toward your Main Quest? If it doesn't, it's just a side quest with no loot.
- **It's Repeatable:** Daily quests need to be simple and consistent. You don't want to spend hours planning them every day—that's like micromanaging your inventory in *Resident Evil*.
- **It's Rewarding:** Choose habits that provide an immediate sense of accomplishment, even if the long-term rewards take time to appear. Think of it like farming gold in *World of Warcraft*—boring at first, but worth it when you finally afford that epic mount.

Examples of Strong Daily Quests:

- Drink water (Stamina Buff).
- Write one paragraph of your novel (Creativity Buff).

- Stretch for five minutes (Agility Buff).
- Read a page of a book (Intelligence Buff).

Pro Tip: Avoid "fetch quests"—the habits that feel like busywork without any real payoff. If your quest doesn't move the needle, it's not worth the grind.

Step 3: Level Up Your Quest Rewards

What's a quest without rewards? Spoiler: it's boring. In gaming, rewards are what keep you grinding, whether it's a legendary weapon drop or a rare card for your collection. In life, rewards are just as crucial, but instead of loot, you're giving yourself tiny boosts of motivation.

Here's how to create a reward system that actually works:

1. **Match the Reward to the Effort:** Big quests deserve big rewards. Finished a major project? Celebrate with something special, like a night out or a new gadget. Smaller quests can get smaller rewards, like a piece of chocolate or 15 minutes of guilt-free gaming.
2. **Make Rewards Immediate:** The human brain is terrible at delayed gratification. If you want your reward system to stick, make sure the payoff happens as soon as the quest is complete.
3. **Use Loot Crates (Without the Predatory Pricing):** Create a mystery box of small rewards—things like snacks, stickers, or gift cards—and pull one out whenever you hit a milestone. It's silly, but it works.

Pro Tip: Don't turn your rewards into de-buffs. If your "treat" is something that sets you back (e.g., eating an entire pizza after one workout), you're just nerfing your progress.

Step 4: Add Some RNG (Randomized Fun)

In gaming, RNG is the unpredictable element that keeps things exciting. Whether it's a surprise boss fight, a rare loot drop, or an unexpected ally, RNG keeps you on your toes. Adding a little randomness to your habit-building routine can have the same effect.

Here's how to sprinkle some RNG into your daily quests:

- **Mix Up the Order:** Change the sequence of your habits to keep things fresh. For example, if your morning routine is feeling stale, try doing your workout *before* breakfast instead of after.
- **Add Wild Cards:** Create a list of optional "wild card" quests that you can draw from when you're feeling adventurous. Examples: "Try a new recipe," "Take a different route to work," or "Play a board game with friends."
- **Roll the Dice:** Use an actual die (or a random number generator) to determine how many times you'll repeat a task. For example, roll a D6 to decide how many pages to read or how many push-ups to do.

Pro Tip: RNG works best in moderation. Too much randomness can feel chaotic, so make sure your core habits stay consistent.

Step 5: Overcome the Grind Wall

Even the best daily quests can start to feel like a grind after a while. This is known as the "grind wall"—the point where motivation drops, and everything feels like a chore. But don't worry, because every hero hits the grind wall at some point. The key is learning how to climb over it.

Here's your grind wall survival guide:

1. **Focus on the Big Picture:** Remind yourself why you're doing this. What's the Main Quest behind your daily grind? Keeping your endgame in mind makes the process more bearable.

2. **Lean on Your Party:** Let your allies (friends, family, or co-workers) know when you're struggling. They can offer encouragement, accountability, or just a much-needed morale boost.

3. **Initiate a Speedrun:** If the quest feels slow, stop treating it like a grind and start treating it like a Time Trial. Speedrunners play the same levels thousands of times without getting bored because they are focused on optimization.

   -Set a Timer: Can you finish your daily cleaning quest in 15 minutes flat? Can you write that email before your "battle music" playlist ends?

   -Beat Your PB: Track your "Personal Best" times for repetitive tasks. Trying to shave seconds off your record turns a boring slog into an adrenaline-fueled race against the clock.

Pro Tip: Treat the grind wall like a mid-level boss. It's annoying, sure, but it's also a test of your determination. Beat it, and you'll unlock the next stage of your journey.

Coming Up Next: Buffing Consistency

Habits are the foundation of every great life build, but consistency is the glue that holds it all together. Next, we'll dive into advanced strategies for staying consistent, tracking your progress, and avoiding the dreaded "quest abandonment syndrome." Because no one wants to be that player who quits halfway through the campaign. Stay tuned, hero—your next level is just around the corner.

Bio Break: AFK for a Minute!

You've made it past the beginner phase of daily quests, and now we're moving into the hardcore mode: **Consistency.** This is where the real magic happens—or, if you're not careful, where the wheels fall off. Consistency isn't glamorous, and it doesn't come with flashy cinematics or epic boss battles. It's the grind that separates the casual players from the true legends.

Think of consistency as the ultimate buff—it amplifies every habit, every quest, every effort you make. The longer you stay consistent, the stronger the effect. Miss too many days, though, and you risk losing the buff entirely. But don't worry, because this part of the chapter is all about teaching you how to maintain your streaks, troubleshoot setbacks, and keep the grind going—even when life tries to nerf your progress.

Step 6: Treat Consistency Like a Dungeon Run

Let's start with a simple truth: consistency is a team effort. Even if your quest is a solo mission, you need the right strategy, tools, and mindset to keep going. Think of it like running a dungeon in *World of Warcraft*—you need to prepare, plan, and execute if you want to survive the grind and reap the rewards.

Here's how to approach consistency like a dungeon run:

1. **Plan Your Route:** Before you start, map out your path. What are the key habits you need to maintain, and what obstacles might you face?
2. **Bring the Right Gear:** Equip yourself with the tools you need to succeed—whether that's a habit-tracking app, a supportive accountability buddy, or just a killer playlist to keep you motivated.
3. **Watch Your Stamina Bar:** Don't burn yourself out by taking on too much at once. Pace yourself, and make sure you're recharging between quests.

Pro Tip: Just like a good dungeon run, consistency is all about preparation. The more you plan ahead, the less likely you are to wipe when things get tough.

Step 7: Use Checkpoints to Stay on Track

Every great game has checkpoints—those critical moments where your progress is saved, and you can catch your breath before diving into the next challenge. In life, checkpoints are just as important for maintaining consistency.

Here's how to set up your own checkpoints:

1. **Weekly Reviews:** At the end of each week, review your progress. What quests did you complete? What could you improve? Treat this as your personal save point.
2. **Monthly Milestones:** Every month, set a bigger goal to aim for. This gives you something to work toward beyond the daily grind.
3. **Annual Reflections:** Once a year, look back at your overall progress. Celebrate your wins, learn from your setbacks, and adjust your strategy for the next level.

Pro Tip: Checkpoints aren't just for tracking progress—they're also for recharging. Use them as a chance to reflect, reset, and refocus your efforts.

Step 8: Master the Art of Resetting

Even the best players need to reset sometimes. Maybe life throws a curveball, or maybe you just lose steam. Whatever the reason, learning how to reset is a critical skill for staying consistent in the long run.

Here's your reset guide:

1. **Acknowledge the Setback:** Pretending it didn't happen won't help. Own your failure, and use it as motivation to do better.
2. **Start Small:** When resetting a habit, go back to basics. Focus on rebuilding your streak one day at a time.
3. **Reassess Your Strategy:** If the habit wasn't working, figure out why. Was it too ambitious? Too boring? Adjust your approach to make it more sustainable.

Pro Tip: Think of resets as respawns. You might lose a little progress, but you're still in the game. And sometimes, a fresh start is exactly what you need to get back on track.

Step 9: Celebrate Your Long-Term Wins

In gaming, the grind is always worth it when you hit a major milestone—whether it's unlocking a legendary weapon, finishing a tough raid, or finally beating that one boss that kept killing you. In life, your long-term wins deserve just as much celebration.

Here's how to celebrate like a pro:

1. **Create a Victory Ritual:** Whether it's treating yourself to a fancy dinner, buying that game you've been eyeing, or just doing a little victory dance, find a way to mark the occasion.
2. **Share Your Wins:** Let your allies know about your accomplishments. They'll cheer you on and maybe even feel inspired to tackle their own quests.
3. **Reflect on Your Progress:** Take a moment to look back at how far you've come. You're not the same player who started this journey, and that's worth celebrating.

Pro Tip: Don't let success make you complacent. Every win is a stepping stone to the next challenge. Stay hungry, and keep leveling up.

Step 10: Set Up Macros and Keybinds (Remove the Friction)

In competitive gaming, the difference between a win and a loss often comes down to speed. That's why pros don't click through five different menus to cast a spell—they set up **Macros** and **Keybinds**. These are shortcuts that execute complex actions with a single button press.

In life, friction is the enemy of consistency. If you have to spend 20 minutes finding your running shoes, searching for your headphones, and clearing space in the living room before you work out, you're playing with terrible "input lag." By the time you're ready to start, your motivation meter has already depleted.

Here's how to set up Macros to make your daily quests effortless:

- **Pre-Load the Assets:** Just like a game loads textures before the level starts, you need to prep your environment ahead of time. Want to run in the morning? Put your clothes, shoes, and water bottle next to your bed the night before. You're essentially creating a "one-click" start for your habit.
- **Optimize Your Hotbar:** Keep the tools you need for your habits in your immediate line of sight (your real-life hotbar). If you want to read more, leave the book on your pillow. If you want to floss, put the floss on top of the toothpaste, not buried in a drawer.
- **Clear the Path:** Remove obstacles that increase the difficulty rating of your quest. If you're trying to eat healthier, delete the food delivery apps from your phone (or at least move them off the home screen). Don't make your character pathfind through a swamp of distractions to get to the objective.

Pro Tip: Think of this as lowering the "activation energy" for your quests. The fewer buttons you have to press to get started, the more likely you are to actually play.

Getting Back Up

Every time you get back up after a failure—whether in life or in a game—you're reinforcing a powerful mental habit. Here's why: when you push through setbacks and finally succeed, your brain rewards you with an even bigger dopamine hit than if you'd succeeded on the first try.

Games are designed to take advantage of this. That's why the hardest bosses drop the best loot and why overcoming a challenging puzzle feels so satisfying. In real life, you can create the same motivational loop by reframing failure as part of the process. Each retry isn't a setback—it's a step closer to that sweet dopamine rush waiting for you when you finally nail it.

Consistency Is Your Ultimate Power-Up

At the end of the day, consistency is what transforms ordinary players into legends. It's not flashy, and it doesn't come with instant gratification, but it's the one skill that guarantees progress over time. By mastering the art of daily quests and staying consistent, you're setting yourself up for long-term success—no cheats, no shortcuts, just pure, hard-earned victory.

In the next chapter, we'll tackle the fine art of tracking your XP and building a reward system that motivates you. Because what's the point of grinding if you're not collecting loot along the way? Get ready to take your quest log to the next level, hero. The journey continues!

Chapter 4: Game Settings - Customizing Your Difficulty

Here's something most self-help books won't tell you: you're probably playing on the wrong difficulty setting.

Maybe you picked "Nightmare Mode" because you thought suffering builds character. Maybe you're stuck on "Easy" because you're terrified of failure. Or maybe—and this is the most common—you've been grinding on "Hard" for so long that you've forgotten there's even a settings menu.

I see this all the time. Someone fresh out of college tries to launch a startup, train for a marathon, learn Japanese, and maintain a perfect social life—all simultaneously. They're playing on Legendary difficulty with starter gear and wondering why they keep respawning at the checkpoint. Or the opposite: someone capable of crushing it instead plays it safe, setting goals so easy that completion feels hollow, wondering why "success" doesn't feel like victory.

Here's the truth that every gamer knows but most people forget when they exit the game: **difficulty settings exist for a reason.** They let you calibrate challenge to your current skill level, available resources, and external circumstances. The best games let you adjust mid-campaign when you realize you bit off more than you can chew—or when you're breezing through content that should be challenging.

Life has the same feature. Most people just don't know how to access the menu.

This chapter is your guide to calibrating your life's difficulty settings. We're going to cover how to recognize when you're playing on the wrong level, how to adjust challenges to maintain that sweet spot between boredom and burnout, and—most importantly—how to give yourself permission to change settings when circumstances shift. Because playing on Hard Mode doesn't make you heroic. It just makes you tired.

Step 1: Understand the Difficulty Spectrum

In gaming, difficulty settings typically range from "Story Mode" (basically interactive movies) to "Nightmare" (where even tutorial enemies can one-shot you). Each serves a purpose. Story Mode lets you enjoy narrative without mechanical stress. Nightmare Mode tests mastery and provides bragging rights.

Life works similarly, except most people never consciously choose their setting—they just default to whatever their parents, society, or their own neuroses programmed into them.

Here's the spectrum:

Tutorial Mode: You're going through the motions with minimal challenge. Safe, comfortable, but ultimately unfulfilling. This is staying in a job you've mastered years ago, dating someone you're not really into because it's convenient, or setting goals you know you'll hit without effort.

Normal Mode: Appropriate challenge for your current skill level. You're stretched but not overwhelmed. Success requires effort but feels achievable. This is the sweet spot for most of life—hard enough to grow, easy enough to maintain.

Hard Mode: Significant challenge that pushes your limits. Success is possible but demands full commitment. This is appropriate for specific growth periods or major goals, but unsustainable long-term.

Nightmare Mode: Borderline impossible given your current resources and circumstances. This is where most burnout happens. You're not building character; you're grinding yourself into dust.

Pro Tip: Most high achievers think they should always play on Nightmare Mode. That's not ambition—that's self-sabotage with better marketing.

Step 2: Recognize When You're on the Wrong Difficulty

The game gives you feedback about difficulty calibration. You just have to pay attention to the signals.

Signs You're Playing Too Easy:

- You're constantly bored and checking out mentally
- Wins feel hollow—like participation trophies, not achievements
- You're not learning anything new or developing skills
- You daydream about bigger challenges but never pursue them
- Deep down, you know you're capable of more but you're playing it safe

Signs You're Playing Too Hard:

- Everything feels like an uphill battle with no respite
- You're constantly exhausted, even after rest
- Small setbacks feel catastrophic
- You fantasize about escape or giving up entirely
- Your health, relationships, or mental state are deteriorating
- You're not making progress despite maximum effort

The Sweet Spot Indicators:

- You're challenged but not overwhelmed
- Wins feel earned and satisfying
- You're growing but not breaking
- You have energy for both work and life
- Setbacks are frustrating but manageable

- You're engaged, not just enduring

Pro Tip: If Monday mornings fill you with existential dread, you're not playing on the right difficulty for your current build.

I learned this the hard way when I took on a massive project while my wife Izzy was dealing with a health crisis. I thought I could just "power through" by playing harder. Spoiler alert: I couldn't. I was playing on Nightmare difficulty with a full-time job, trying to support my partner, and launching something that required 60-hour weeks. The game didn't care about my determination—it just kept wiping me until I finally adjusted the settings.

Step 3: Master the Flow State Sweet Spot

Psychologist Mihály Csíkszentmihályi spent his career studying optimal challenge—that magical state where you're fully immersed, time disappears, and you're performing at your peak. He called it "flow."

Flow happens in a narrow band: when challenge slightly exceeds skill, but not by so much that it triggers anxiety. Too easy, and you're bored. Too hard, and you're stressed. Just right, and you're in the zone.

The Flow Channel:

- **Skill Level:** Where you are now
- **Challenge Level:** What you're attempting
- **Flow Zone:** Challenge is 4-10% above current skill

How to find your flow zone:

Assess Current Capabilities Honestly: Not where you wish you were. Not where you used to be. Where you actually are right now, with your current resources, energy, and circumstances.

Add Incremental Challenge: Increase difficulty by small margins—enough to stretch, not enough to snap. If you can run a 5K, train for a 10K, not a marathon.

Monitor Your State: Are you engaged or overwhelmed? Growing or grinding? Adjust accordingly.

Adjust Based on External Factors: Your optimal difficulty changes when circumstances change. New baby? Dial it down. Just got promoted with new bandwidth? Dial it up.

Pro Tip: Flow state doesn't mean everything is easy—it means everything is possible. If "possible" is starting to feel like "maybe with divine intervention," you've overshot the zone.

Step 4: Recognize "Hard Mode" Thinking (And Why It's Sabotage)

There's a toxic belief floating around hustle culture: if it's not brutally difficult, you're not trying hard enough. That success requires suffering. That ease is somehow shameful.

This is garbage.

Common Hard Mode Fallacies:

"If I'm not exhausted, I'm not working hard enough." (Burnout isn't a badge of honor—it's a bug in your system.)

"I should be able to handle everything everyone else handles." (Everyone else is lying about how much they're handling.)

"Adjusting difficulty downward is quitting." (No. Quitting is when you stop playing. Adjusting settings is strategic optimization.)

"Successful people don't need easy modes." (Successful people are extremely good at identifying what to make easy so they can focus energy where it matters.)

"If I make things easier, I'm weak." (If you deliberately make things harder for no reason, you're not strong—you're inefficient.)

The Reality:

Hard Mode has its place—specific challenges, growth sprints, important goals. But living permanently on Hard Mode doesn't build character. It builds resentment, exhaustion, and eventual collapse.

The strongest players aren't the ones grinding on Nightmare difficulty with broken gear. They're the ones who know when to dial difficulty up for growth and when to dial it down for sustainability.

Pro Tip: If your current strategy involves pretending you don't have limits, your strategy is bad. Every character has a stamina bar. Ignoring it doesn't make you tough—it makes you sidelined.

Step 5: Scale Goals to Current Life Circumstances

Your life circumstances aren't static. New job. Relationship changes. Health issues. Family demands. Financial stress. Any major life transition changes your available resources—time, energy, focus, money.

Most people's mistake? They set goals during optimal conditions, then refuse to adjust when circumstances shift. That's like starting a game on Normal, having the difficulty spike to Nightmare without warning, and insisting you can still maintain the same pace.

How to scale intelligently:

Acknowledge Life Phases: Some seasons are for aggressive growth. Others are for maintenance. Both are valid. A new parent isn't "less ambitious"—they're allocating resources to a critically important quest.

Identify Non-Negotiables: What absolutely must continue? Health basics? Key relationships? Core work commitments? Everything else is negotiable.

Adjust the Scope, Not the Direction: Having a baby doesn't mean abandoning fitness goals—it means "workout 6 days a week" becomes "move your body 15 minutes daily." Same direction, calibrated scope.

Set Conditional Goals: "If X circumstances, then Y goals." This removes guilt when you need to adjust. "During this project deadline, I'm maintaining baseline health, not chasing PRs."

Give Yourself Explicit Permission: "For the next three months, I'm dialing difficulty down to focus on [specific priority]. This is strategic, not weak."

Pro Tip: Your 22-year-old self's capability isn't the permanent baseline. Neither is your "best ever" performance. Context matters. A runner recovering from injury shouldn't judge themselves against their marathon PR—they should celebrate getting back to running at all.

Bio Break: AFK for a Minute!

You've learned to recognize difficulty mismatches, understand flow states, avoid Hard Mode thinking, and scale goals to circumstances. Now let's get into the tactical stuff—how to actually adjust settings across different life domains, handle external vs. self-imposed difficulty, and build sustainable systems that adapt as you level up.

Grab water. Stretch. And let's dive into advanced difficulty calibration.

Step 6: Learn to Adjust Settings in Real-Time

Difficulty adjustment isn't just for major life transitions. Sometimes you need to make tactical changes mid-quest when you realize you've miscalibrated.

How to adjust on the fly:

The Daily Dial: Each morning, honestly assess: How am I actually feeling? What's my energy level? What's happening today? Then adjust your daily quests accordingly. Feeling 90%? Push a bit. Feeling 60%? Maintain baseline. Feeling 30%? Survival mode—do the absolute minimum.

The Weekly Reset: Every week, review what worked and what didn't. If you consistently can't complete your planned tasks, you're playing too hard. If you're breezing through everything, you're playing too easy.

The Emergency Override: Sometimes life throws curveballs—illness, family crisis, unexpected deadline. Give yourself permission to hit pause on growth goals and switch to maintenance mode. No guilt. No shame. Just intelligent resource allocation.

The Gradual Ramp: When increasing difficulty, do it incrementally. Add one challenge at a time. Lock it in for 2-3 weeks. Then consider adding more. This prevents the common mistake of cranking everything to max simultaneously and immediately burning out.

Pro Tip: Your difficulty settings should be as dynamic as your life. Static goals in a dynamic world is a recipe for frustration.

Step 7: Distinguish External vs. Self-Imposed Difficulty

Not all difficulty is created equal. Some challenges are externally imposed—your job demands, economic reality, health conditions, family obligations. Others are self-imposed—the standards you set, the goals you choose, the way you judge yourself.

Understanding the difference is critical because you can't adjust external difficulty much, but you have total control over self-imposed difficulty.

External Difficulty (Limited Control):

- Job requirements and deadlines
- Economic circumstances
- Health challenges
- Family obligations
- Societal expectations that have real consequences

Self-Imposed Difficulty (Full Control):

- The standards you set beyond requirements
- Goals you pursue by choice
- How you interpret setbacks

- The story you tell yourself about what you "should" be able to handle
- Comparison to others' highlight reels

The Trap:

Most people drastically underestimate how much difficulty is self-imposed. Your job might require 40 hours, but you work 60 because you think you should. Your health might require gentle movement, but you push for intense workouts because anything less feels like failure.

The Liberation:

Once you realize how much difficulty is optional, you can make strategic choices. Keep external requirements. Evaluate every self-imposed standard: Is this serving me? Is this timing right? Could I achieve 80% of the benefit with 50% of the effort?

Pro Tip: Ask yourself: "Who told me this should be this hard?" If the answer is "society" or "my anxiety" rather than actual reality, you've found self-imposed difficulty that might need adjustment.

Step 8: Build Difficulty Flexibility Into Your Systems

The best systems don't demand perfection—they accommodate reality. Instead of rigid "all or nothing" approaches, build in difficulty tiers you can adjust based on circumstances.

How to create flexible systems:

The Three-Tier Approach:

For any habit or goal, define three difficulty levels:

- **Baseline (Easy):** Absolute minimum to maintain momentum. Even on terrible days, you can do this. (Example: 5-minute walk)
- **Standard (Normal):** What you aim for on regular days. Challenging but sustainable. (Example: 30-minute workout)

- **Stretch (Hard):** When conditions are optimal and you want to push. (Example: 60-minute intense training)

Then decide daily which tier you're playing.

The Scaling Framework:

Instead of fixed targets, use ranges:

- Writing: 250-1000 words
- Exercise: 15-60 minutes
- Reading: 10-50 pages

Aim for the middle. Hit the low end on hard days. Exceed on good days. Always making progress, never stuck in all-or-nothing thinking.

The Pause Button:

Build in planned difficulty reductions for known stressful periods. Tax season? Maintenance mode. Family visiting? Lower targets. Major project? Reduce non-essential goals proactively.

Pro Tip: Flexible systems are sustainable systems. Rigid systems work great until they don't—then they catastrophically fail. Build in adjustment capability from the start.

Step 9: Give Yourself Permission to Change Settings

This is where most people get stuck. They know they should adjust difficulty, but they feel guilty doing it. Like they're "giving up" or "being weak."

Let me be crystal clear: **Adjusting difficulty settings isn't failure. It's intelligent gameplay.**

Common Permission Blocks:

"I used to handle more." (Different circumstances. Different life stage. Irrelevant comparison.)

"Everyone else seems to manage." (Everyone else is either lying, burning out quietly, or has completely different circumstances than you.)

"I should be able to push through." (Why? Who benefits from you grinding yourself into dust?)

"Adjusting down means I'm not committed." (Adjusting means you're committed to sustainability over performance theater.)

The Permission Framework:

Recognize: Name what's changed. "I have a new baby." "I'm dealing with grief." "My job demands increased." "I'm recovering from burnout."

Accept: This change is real and impacts capacity. Pretending it doesn't won't make it go away.

Adjust: Make specific, explicit changes to goals, standards, or commitments. Write them down.

Commit: To the adjusted version. This is your real goal now, not a consolation prize.

Release: Let go of guilt. You're not "less than"—you're calibrating intelligently.

Pro Tip: The people judging you for adjusting difficulty aren't playing your game. They don't know your stats, your current quests, or your available resources. Their opinions are irrelevant data.

Step 10: Know When to Dial Difficulty Back Up

Adjusting difficulty down is important. But so is recognizing when you're ready to dial it back up. Playing on Easy Mode indefinitely is just as problematic as permanent Hard Mode—you stagnate, get bored, and lose the satisfaction that comes from meaningful challenge.

Signs You're Ready to Increase Difficulty:

- Current challenges feel routine and unchallenging

- You have excess energy and capacity after completing baseline goals
- You're genuinely curious about pushing boundaries
- External circumstances have stabilized
- You're thinking "I could probably handle more"
- The thought of staying at current level feels stifling

How to Scale Up Safely:

Add One Thing: Don't crank everything to max. Add one new challenge or increase one goal by 10-20%. Lock that in for a month.

Monitor Impact: Is it energizing or draining? Building you up or wearing you down? Adjust accordingly.

Celebrate the Stretch: Acknowledge that you've recalibrated upward because you're ready, not because you "should."

Build in Reassessment: Every 4-6 weeks, check in. Still feel good? Consider another small increase. Feeling strained? Hold steady or dial back slightly.

Keep Difficulty Tiers: Even as you scale up, maintain your three-tier system. Your new "Normal" might be your old "Hard," but you still need "Easy" for bad days.

Pro Tip: Difficulty calibration isn't one-and-done. It's continuous optimization. You'll dial up and down throughout your life as circumstances and capacity change. This is normal, healthy, and smart.

Master Your Settings, Master Your Game

Here's what most self-help gurus won't tell you: there is no universal "right" difficulty level. The right difficulty is the one that challenges you appropriately for your current circumstances, resources, and goals—while remaining sustainable

Some seasons of life demand you dial difficulty down—and that's not weakness, it's wisdom. Other seasons offer the capacity to dial up—and that's not obligation, it's opportunity.

The players who win long-term aren't the ones who permanently max out difficulty and grind until they break. They're the ones who continuously calibrate, adjust, adapt, and optimize. They play Hard Mode when they can. They shift to Normal Mode when they should. And they don't apologize for either.

You have permission to:

- Play on Easy when life is hard
- Increase difficulty when you're ready
- Dial it back down when circumstances change
- Ignore anyone who judges your settings
- Prioritize sustainability over performance theater
- Change your mind about what you can handle
- Build a life that works for you, not some imaginary ideal version of you that doesn't exist

The difficulty settings are yours to control. Stop letting default settings, other people's expectations, or outdated versions of yourself dictate how hard your life has to be.

Open the menu. Adjust the settings. Play the game that lets you thrive, not just survive.

Because the goal isn't to prove you can beat the game on Nightmare Mode with broken gear while blindfolded. The goal is to actually enjoy playing—and keep playing long enough to see how the story ends.

Now go recalibrate. Your optimal difficulty is waiting.

Chapter 5: Gaining Experience Points (XP) and Reward Systems

You've made it to Chapter 5, hero, and things are about to get *real.* We're talking about the good stuff now—XP and rewards. The grind is only bearable because of what comes after. Whether it's the sweet loot from a raid, the dopamine hit of leveling up, or the pure satisfaction of checking off a quest, the rewards keep us coming back for more.

But here's the thing about life: it doesn't automatically hand out XP just because you showed up. In fact life's pretty stingy with rewards unless you make a point to track and celebrate your progress. So, in this chapter, we're going to learn how to hack the system. You'll figure out how to track your XP, build a reward system that actually works, and create the ultimate feedback loop to keep yourself motivated.

Step 1: Understand How XP Works in Real Life

In video games, XP is straightforward: kill the enemy, complete the quest, level up. Easy, right? In life, it's not so simple. There's no progress bar hovering over your head, no fanfare when you accomplish something, and no clear way to measure how close you are to leveling up.

So how do you earn XP in real life? By creating your own system. Think of XP as a metaphor for growth—every skill you learn, habit you build, or challenge you conquer earns you experience. But you've got to track it to see your progress.

Here's how to start tracking your real-life XP:

1. **Break Down Your Goals into XP Values:** Assign point values to your tasks based on difficulty. For example, a small task like responding to an email might be worth 5 XP,

while a bigger task like completing a project could be worth 50 XP.

2. **Track Your Daily Gains:** At the end of each day, tally up your XP. You can use a notebook, an app, or even a custom spreadsheet (bonus points for adding cool graphics).
3. **Set Level-Up Thresholds:** Decide how much XP you need to hit before leveling up. Maybe every 500 XP equals a level—whatever feels right for your personal game.

Pro Tip: Treat your XP system like a tabletop RPG—customize it to fit your goals, and make it fun to use. If it starts to feel like a chore, tweak it until it doesn't.

Step 2: Build a Reward System That Actually Works

XP is great and all, but the real reason we grind is for the rewards. In gaming, rewards come in all shapes and sizes—loot, badges, achievements, you name it. In life, your rewards system is just as important, and the key is to make it both satisfying and sustainable.

Here's how to build a reward system that keeps you motivated:

1. **Match Rewards to the Task:** The bigger the quest, the bigger the reward. If you're tackling a massive project, treat yourself to something epic when it's done (Covered in Chapter 3).
2. **Include Surprise Drops:** Add a little RNG (random number generator) magic to your rewards. For example, create a "loot box" of rewards (like gift cards, treats, or mini-breaks) and randomly pick one whenever you hit a milestone.
3. **Avoid Counterproductive Rewards:** If your reward undoes your progress (e.g., bingeing junk food after a workout), it's a de-buff, not a buff. Choose rewards that enhance your progress instead of derailing it.

Pro Tip: Think of rewards as buffs—they should make you stronger, happier, or more motivated. If a reward feels more like a de-buff, ditch it and find something better.

Step 3: Gamify Your Progress Tracking

One of the best things about video games is the constant feedback. Whether it's a level-up animation, a shiny new piece of gear, or just the satisfying *ping* of an achievement unlocking, you always know how you're doing. Real life? Not so much. That's why it's up to you to create your own feedback loop.

Here's how to gamify your progress tracking:

1. **Create a Progress Bar:** Whether it's a physical chart, a digital tracker, or even just a doodle in your notebook, find a way to visually represent your progress. Watching your XP bar fill up is surprisingly satisfying.
2. **Set Achievement Milestones:** Build a list of achievements to unlock as you progress. Examples: "Write 10,000 words" (Achievement: Wordsmith) or "Go to the gym 30 days in a row" (Achievement: Fitness Buff).
3. **Use Leaderboards:** If you're feeling competitive, create a leaderboard with friends, family, or co-workers. A little friendly competition can go a long way in keeping everyone motivated.

Pro Tip: Keep it fun. If your progress tracker starts to feel like homework, you're doing it wrong. Add stickers, colors, or memes to keep things lighthearted.

Step 4: Reward Progress, Not Just Results

In gaming, you don't only get rewards at the end of the quest—you're constantly earning smaller rewards along the way. Life works the same way. If you only reward yourself for hitting massive milestones, you'll burn out before you get there.

Here's how to reward progress:

1. **Celebrate Small Wins:** Every step forward deserves recognition. Finished a tough email? That's a win. Took the stairs instead of the elevator? Another win.
2. **Create Mid-Quest Checkpoints:** For bigger goals, break them into smaller milestones and reward yourself at each checkpoint.
3. **Practice Gratitude:** Sometimes the reward is just acknowledging how far you've come. Take a moment to appreciate your own efforts—it's cheesy, but it works.

Pro Tip: Think of progress rewards as health potions. They might seem small, but they're what keep you alive during the grind.

Step 5: Watch Out for XP Sinkholes

Not all XP is created equal. Just like in games, some tasks might feel productive but don't actually move the needle. These are the XP sinkholes—the tasks that eat up your time without giving you much in return.

Here's how to avoid XP sinkholes:

1. **Prioritize High-Value Tasks:** Focus on the quests that align with your Main Quest. Busywork might feel satisfying in the moment, but it's not worth the grind.
2. **Track Your Time:** If you're not sure where your time is going, use a time-tracking app to identify the sinkholes.
3. **Learn to Say No:** If a quest doesn't fit your priorities, it's okay to skip it. Not every NPC needs your help.

Pro Tip: Treat XP sinkholes like bad loot drops. Learn to spot them early, and don't waste your energy grinding for something that won't pay off.

Coming Up Next: The Loot You Deserve

Now that you've mastered the art of tracking your XP and building a reward system, it's time to dive deeper into the loot. Next, we'll explore how to turn your achievements into tangible rewards, create a legacy of progress, and keep the grind exciting even when the game gets tough. Because if you're not collecting loot, what's the point of playing?

Bio Break: AFK for a Minute!

By now, you're tracking your XP like a pro, celebrating small wins, and avoiding the dreaded XP sinkholes. But what good is all this grinding if you don't get some loot to show for it? This section is all about collecting the rewards you deserve, creating a system that keeps you motivated, and making sure your grind doesn't feel like the most boring side quest in a bad RPG.

Because if life's a game, then loot is the whole point. And whether your loot comes in the form of money, achievements, or just the sweet satisfaction of beating the odds, you deserve every bit of it.

Step 6: Define Your Loot Goals

In gaming, loot comes in all shapes and sizes: epic weapons, rare armor, shiny gold coins. In life, loot is whatever gives you a sense of accomplishment or joy. The trick is knowing what kind of loot matters most to you and focusing your efforts on quests that deliver it.

Here's how to define your loot goals:

1. **Identify Your "Legendary Gear":** What's your ultimate reward? A dream vacation? Financial freedom? A fully maxed-out gaming rig? Whatever it is, write it down and make it your endgame loot.
2. **Add Mid-Level Rewards:** Not every quest leads to legendary gear, and that's okay. Mid-level loot—like a night out, a new book, or a weekend getaway—is just as important for keeping you motivated.
3. **Include Consumables:** Think of these as your short-term rewards, like health potions in an RPG. Examples include a

cup of coffee, an hour of gaming, or a guilt-free Netflix binge.

Pro Tip: Don't get distracted by "junk loot." If a reward doesn't align with your goals or values, it's just clutter in your inventory.

Step 7: Turn Achievements Into Tangible Rewards

Unlocking achievements is great, but digital badges don't pay the bills. That's why it's important to turn your real-life achievements into tangible rewards. Think of this as converting your in-game currency into something you can actually use.

Here's how to do it:

1. **Monetize Your Skills:** If you've leveled up a marketable skill, find a way to turn it into income. For example, if you've been grinding your writing XP, start freelancing or self-publishing.
2. **Invest in Your Growth:** Use your rewards to fund your future progress. That might mean taking a course, upgrading your gear (literally or figuratively), or even hiring a coach or mentor.
3. **Celebrate Big Wins:** When you hit a major milestone, treat yourself to something you've been dreaming about. This isn't just about indulgence—it's about reinforcing the idea that your hard work pays off.

Pro Tip: Think of tangible rewards as artifacts from your journey. Every item should remind you of what you accomplished to earn it.

Step 8: Create a Legacy of Progress

In gaming, your legacy is the mark you leave behind—the high scores, the speedrun records, the fully completed save files. In life, your legacy is the lasting impact of your efforts. It's not just about what you achieve; it's about how your progress benefits you and others in the long run.

Here's how to build a legacy of progress:

1. **Document Your Journey:** Keep a journal, blog, or social media account where you track your achievements and share your story. Not only does this create a record of your progress, but it can also inspire others.

2. **Pay It Forward:** Share your knowledge, skills, and resources with others. Whether it's mentoring someone, teaching a class, or just offering advice, helping others is the ultimate legacy.

3. **Focus on Long-Term Goals:** While short-term rewards are great, your legacy is built on the big-picture achievements. Keep your eyes on the Main Quest, even as you enjoy the smaller wins along the way.

Pro Tip: Legacy isn't about being remembered—it's about creating something that lasts. Every time you level up, think about how your progress can make a difference beyond yourself.

Step 9: Keep the Grind Fun

Let's be honest: even the best games can start to feel repetitive if you're grinding the same quest over and over. That's why it's crucial to keep your grind fun, fresh, and engaging. If you're not enjoying the journey, you're doing it wrong.

Here's how to keep the grind exciting:

1. **Add Variety:** Mix up your quests to keep things interesting. If your routine is starting to feel stale, swap out one habit for something new.

2. **Challenge Yourself:** Set stretch goals that push you outside your comfort zone. Just like a challenging raid boss, these quests are tough but rewarding.

3. **Find Joy in the Process:** Sometimes, the best rewards aren't tangible—they're the sense of pride and accomplishment that comes from giving your all.

Pro Tip: Treat your grind like a co-op game. Bring friends along for the ride, and share the experience. Everything's more fun with a party.

Step 10: Balance Loot with Life

Here's the thing about loot: it's only valuable if it adds to your life instead of taking over it. Chasing rewards is great, but don't forget to enjoy the game itself. After all, what's the point of earning all that gold if you never stop to spend it?

Here's how to strike the right balance:

1. **Define "Enough":** Decide what success looks like for you, and don't get caught up in endless grinding just for the sake of it.
2. **Enjoy the Moment:** Take time to appreciate where you are, even if you haven't hit your ultimate goal yet. Every level is worth celebrating.
3. **Avoid Burnout:** If you're feeling overwhelmed, it's okay to step back and take a break. Life isn't a speedrun—it's a marathon.

Pro Tip: Think of balance as the ultimate loot—it's rare, valuable, and absolutely worth the effort to find.

Your Habits Reward You

Think of your brain like a game developer—it loves designing habits around systems that reward you. When you complete a small quest, like writing 500 words a day or hitting the gym, and immediately reward yourself, you're building a habit loop. The task becomes less about the grind and more about the dopamine hit you get at the end.

In gaming, this is called a reward cycle. In life, it's called habit formation. By creating mini-rewards for every milestone—like a coffee after a workout or 15 minutes of gaming after finishing your work—you're essentially programming your brain to associate effort with satisfaction. Over time, the habit becomes second nature, and motivation becomes automatic."*

The Grind Never Ends (and That's a Good Thing)

At the end of the day, life's grind is what makes it meaningful. The XP you earn, the loot you collect, and the progress you make all add up to something greater than the sum of their parts. By tracking your XP, building a reward system, and staying focused on what matters most, you're not just playing the game—you're winning it.

In the next chapter, we'll tackle the ultimate challenge: overcoming obstacles and boss battles. Because no matter how strong you are or how epic your gear is, every hero faces tough fights. And trust me, you're going to need all the buffs you can get.

Chapter 6: Overcoming Obstacles and Boss Battles

Ah, boss battles. The ultimate test of your strength, strategy, and patience. Whether it's the final showdown with Sephiroth, the grueling grind of *Elden Ring,* or your first attempt at family Thanksgiving as an adult, boss battles are where legends are made.

In life, obstacles and challenges are your bosses. They come in all shapes and sizes, from minor nuisances (like a Monday morning meeting) to massive, soul-crushing behemoths (like that one life crisis you're still trying to forget). But here's the thing: no matter how tough the boss, there's always a strategy to beat it.

This chapter is all about helping you conquer those boss battles. We'll cover everything from preparing for the fight to learning from your losses. Because let's be honest, you're going to take some hits—it's not *God Mode* out here. But with the right tools, mindset, and maybe a little luck, you'll come out on top.

Step 1: Scout the Boss

Every great boss fight starts with intel. You wouldn't charge into a raid without knowing the mechanics, and you shouldn't tackle life's challenges without doing your homework. Scouting the boss is about understanding what you're up against and preparing accordingly.

Here's how to scout your real-life bosses:

1. **Identify the Challenge:** What exactly are you facing? Is it a big work project, a difficult conversation, or a personal setback?
2. **Understand the Mechanics:** Break the challenge into smaller parts. What are the key obstacles, and what strategies might work against them?

3. **Assess the Risk:** How bad will it be if you fail? Knowing the stakes will help you decide how much energy and focus to invest in the fight.

Pro Tip: Treat this like a strategy guide. The more you know about the boss, the better your chances of success.

Step 2: Gear Up for the Fight

No one takes on a boss with starter gear—unless they're doing some kind of masochistic challenge run. Before you face your obstacle, make sure you've equipped yourself with the right tools, resources, and allies.

Here's how to gear up:

1. **Equip Your Skills:** What abilities do you need to succeed? If you're tackling a professional challenge, that might mean brushing up on a specific skill. If it's a physical goal, it might mean building strength or endurance.
2. **Stock Your Inventory:** Gather the resources you need to handle the challenge. This could be anything from research materials to emotional support snacks.
3. **Recruit Your Party:** Some bosses require backup. Don't be afraid to call in allies who can help you tackle the challenge.

Pro Tip: Don't forget your consumables. Just like potions in an RPG, things like rest, nutrition, and self-care can make a huge difference during a tough fight.

Step 3: Study the Patterns

If you've ever fought a boss in a game, you know that every enemy has patterns. They telegraph their moves, repeat certain behaviors, and usually have a weak spot you can exploit. Real-life bosses are no different.

Here's how to study the patterns:

1. **Look for Repeats:** What behaviors or obstacles keep showing up? For example, if you're dealing with a difficult co-worker, do they always react a certain way in meetings?
2. **Find the Weak Spot:** Every challenge has a vulnerability. Maybe your boss battle is a work deadline, and the weak spot is better time management. Find the weak link and focus your efforts there.
3. **Adapt Your Strategy:** Once you know the patterns, adjust your approach. Just like dodging a boss's one-hit KO attack, timing and precision are everything.

Pro Tip: Think of this step as the "trial and error" phase. Don't get discouraged if it takes a few tries to figure out the boss's moves.

Step 4: Use Your Buffs and De-Buffs Wisely

In every game, buffs and de-buffs are the secret weapons that can turn the tide of a battle. Buffs make you stronger, faster, or more resilient, while de-buffs weaken your enemies. In life, these mechanics are just as important.

Here's how to use buffs and de-buffs in real life:

1. **Buff Yourself:** Before tackling a challenge, stack your buffs. This could mean boosting your confidence with positive affirmations, sharpening your focus with a clear plan, or simply getting a good night's sleep.
2. **De-Buff the Boss:** Find ways to weaken the challenge. For example, if you're overwhelmed by a big project, break it into smaller tasks to make it more manageable.
3. **Avoid Self-De-Buffs:** Watch out for habits or behaviors that weaken you, like procrastination, negative self-talk, or staying up too late binge-watching your favorite show.

Pro Tip: Treat this like potion management—use your buffs strategically, and don't waste them on minor encounters.

Step 5: Learn to Take the Hits

Here's the hard truth: no matter how well-prepared you are, you're going to take some hits. Boss battles are designed to test you, and failure is part of the process. The key is learning how to recover and keep going.

Here's how to take the hits:

1. **Use Your Shields:** When things get tough, rely on your defenses. This could mean leaning on your support network, taking a mental health day, or simply stepping back to regroup.
2. **Heal Between Rounds:** After a tough fight, take time to heal. Reflect on what went wrong, and use it as a learning opportunity for the next attempt.
3. **Keep Moving:** No matter how many times you fall, the only way to lose is to stop trying. Pick yourself up, dust yourself off, and get back in the game.

Pro Tip: Treat every hit as an XP gain. Even when you fail, you're still learning, growing, and leveling up.

Boss Battles Are Where Heroes Are Made

Every epic story has a turning point—a moment when the hero faces a challenge so big, so impossible, that it feels like the end. But it's not the end. It's just the beginning of your rise to greatness. Boss battles aren't just obstacles—they're opportunities to prove what you're capable of.

Next, we'll dive deeper into advanced boss-busting strategies, including how to handle unexpected mechanics, deal with multiple bosses at once, and use your losses as fuel for your next victory. Every hero has to lose a few times before they win.

Bio Break: AFK for a Minute!

You've scouted the boss, geared up, studied the patterns, stacked your buffs, and braced yourself for impact. But what happens when the boss fight doesn't go as planned? What do you do when the mechanics change mid-fight, or when a second boss shows up uninvited, pulling aggro just as you're getting the hang of things?

In this section, we'll cover advanced boss-busting strategies to help you stay cool under pressure, adapt to unexpected challenges, and turn your losses into XP for the next round. Because life doesn't always follow the script—and neither do the toughest bosses.

Step 6: Adapt to Unexpected Mechanics

In gaming, surprise mechanics are the worst. One minute you're dodging fireballs, and the next, the boss is summoning minions or unleashing a phase-two attack that wasn't in the walkthrough. In life, unexpected mechanics show up as curveballs: a sudden deadline, an unforeseen expense, or a global pandemic (yeah, *that* boss was a doozy).

Here's how to handle surprise mechanics like a pro:

1. **Pause and Assess:** When the fight changes, don't panic. Take a moment to figure out what's happening and adjust your strategy accordingly.
2. **Stay Flexible:** Be willing to pivot. If your original plan isn't working, try a different approach. For example, if a conversation with a difficult coworker isn't going well, switch tactics—maybe humor or empathy is the key.
3. **Use Emergency Skills:** Every hero has a few emergency skills for when things go sideways. These might include calling a mentor, delegating tasks, or simply stepping away for a breather.

Pro Tip: Treat surprises like bonus stages. They're frustrating, sure, but they're also an opportunity to show off your adaptability.

Step 7: Handle Multiple Bosses at Once

Every gamer dreads the multi-boss fight. It's chaotic, overwhelming, and downright unfair—just like juggling multiple challenges in real life. But with the right strategy, even the most hectic fights can be managed.

Here's how to handle multiple bosses:

1. **Prioritize Targets:** Focus on the boss that's causing the most damage first. If one challenge is draining your energy or resources, take it down before moving on to the next.
2. **Crowd Control:** Find ways to minimize distractions. In gaming, this might mean stunning or freezing lesser enemies. In life, it might mean setting boundaries or delegating tasks.
3. **Use AOE (Area of Effect) Skills:** Look for solutions that tackle multiple challenges at once. For example, improving your time management can help you handle both work and personal responsibilities more efficiently.

Pro Tip: Treat multi-boss fights like puzzles. The chaos might seem overwhelming at first, but with patience and strategy you can break it down into manageable pieces.

Step 8: Learn from the Wipe

In gaming, wiping is part of the process. No one beats a tough boss on the first try (unless they're some kind of speedrunning prodigy). The same is true in life. Failure isn't the end—it's just another step on the path to victory.

Here's how to learn from your losses:

1. **Analyze What Went Wrong:** After a failed attempt, take a step back and figure out what happened. Did you underestimate the challenge? Were you unprepared? Did you run out of stamina halfway through?
2. **Adjust Your Strategy:** Use what you learned to refine your approach. Maybe you need to level up a specific skill or call in reinforcements for the next attempt.

3. **Keep Trying:** The only way to truly fail is to stop trying. Every wipe is a chance to come back stronger, smarter, and more determined.

Pro Tip: Think of failure as XP. Every time you lose, you're gaining the knowledge and experience you need to win.

Step 9: Use Power-Ups and Breaks Strategically

Every tough fight requires strategic use of power-ups. In gaming, these might be health potions, damage boosts, or invincibility stars. In life, your power-ups are the things that recharge your energy and give you an edge.

Here's how to use them wisely:

1. **Time Your Power-Ups:** Don't waste your energy boost on minor tasks. Save your focus and effort for when you need it most, like during a big presentation or a crucial conversation.
2. **Take Breaks:** Just like in games, stepping away from the fight can give you a fresh perspective. A short walk, a quick nap, or even a round of your favorite card game can help you recharge.
3. **Celebrate Small Victories:** Even if you're not done with the fight, take a moment to acknowledge your progress. Each small win is a boost to your morale.

Pro Tip: Treat power-ups like limited resources. Use them when it matters, and don't forget to restock when you're running low.

Step 10: Celebrate the Win (and Prepare for the Next Fight)

Beating a boss is one of the most satisfying moments in any game, but the story doesn't end there. Another boss will always show up eventually, and the grind continues. That's why it's important to celebrate your victories *and* use them as a springboard for future success.

Here's how to do it:

1. **Acknowledge Your Growth:** Take a moment to reflect on how far you've come. What skills did you level up? What strategies worked?
2. **Share the Victory:** Let your allies know about your win. Not only will they celebrate with you, but they might also learn from your experience.
3. **Prepare for the Next Challenge:** Use your momentum to tackle the next big obstacle. Each boss you beat is proof that you can handle whatever comes next.

Pro Tip: Treat your victories like save points. Celebrate them, but don't get complacent—there's always another chapter to play.

Every Boss Is Beat-Able

Let's get real—nobody defeats a boss on their first try unless they're a glitch-abusing speed runner. For the rest of us, failure is just part of the process. It's how we learn the mechanics, spot the patterns, and figure out the timing. Every wipe, every 'You Died' screen, is a step closer to victory because it gives you the data you need to improve.

In life, failure works the same way. You'll mess up. A lot. But every misstep is just another attempt logged, another chance to refine your strategy. Think of failure as an unsaved checkpoint—annoying, sure, but not permanent. With every restart, you come back stronger, smarter, and more prepared to crush the challenge ahead.

Boss Battles Exist in Life

Boss battles aren't limited to video games. Think about the final rounds in *Clue*, where you're trying to piece together who did it, where, and with what weapon. Or the tense moments in *Catan* when someone builds the longest road, tipping the scales in their favor.

But let's be honest: you didn't pick up this book to get better at board games. In the real world, boss battles rarely look like monsters. Instead, they manifest as **Gatekeepers**—high-stakes moments that block your path to the next level.

It's that job interview where the interviewer feels like a Level 50 Raid Boss. It's the crushing debt that requires a long-term resource management strategy to defeat. Or maybe it's that one difficult conversation you've been dodging, the one that drains your stamina just thinking about it. These are the moments that test whether you've actually learned the mechanics or if you've just been button-mashing through your daily routine.

Every Boss is Beatable

No matter how impossible a challenge seems, remember this: every boss is beatable. It might take time, strategy, and a few resets, but with the right approach, you'll come out on top. The obstacles in your path aren't there to stop you, they're there to show you what you're capable of.

In the next chapter, we'll focus on building your support network. Because even the greatest heroes can't do it alone, and a strong party can make all the difference when the going gets tough. Until then, keep grinding, keep learning, and keep proving that you're the hero of your own story.

Chapter 7: Multiplayer Mode — Building Your Party and Crushing Bosses Together

Here's something every hardcore solo player eventually learns: the best loot is behind the co-op door. You can grind for hours, optimize your build to perfection, and still hit a wall that no amount of skill can break through alone. Some dungeons require a healer. Some bosses need a tank to draw aggro. And some quests? They're simply impossible without a full party watching your back.

Life works the same way. Even the most self-reliant among us—the lone wolves who pride themselves on independence—eventually realize that the biggest achievements require other people. Not just any people, though. The right people. A carefully assembled team of allies who complement your strengths, cover your weaknesses, and make the whole journey infinitely more rewarding.

This chapter is your complete guide to multiplayer mode. We're going to cover how to recruit the right party members, build unshakeable synergy, tackle epic challenges together, and leave a legacy that inspires future players. Because the truth is, solo runs make for good stories, but the legendary victories? Those happen when your guild shows up ready to fight.

Step 1: Understand Why Multiplayer Isn't Optional

Before we dive into team-building strategies, let's address the elephant in the raid room: why bother? If you're capable and driven, why not just solo everything?

Here's the uncomfortable truth: solo players hit ceilings. There are hard limits to what one person can accomplish, no matter how talented. Teams multiply your capabilities. They bring perspectives you don't have, skills you haven't developed, and energy when yours runs out.

Think about the greatest achievements in gaming. World-first raid completions. Tournament championships. Speedrun world records held by relay teams. None of them happen alone. The same applies to life—startups need co-founders, projects need collaborators, and even the most introverted creative needs an editor, a mentor, or at least someone to tell them when their idea is terrible.

Here's what a strong party gives you:

Complementary Skills: You can't be great at everything. A balanced party covers gaps you didn't even know you had. Your big-picture visionary needs a detail-oriented executor. Your technical wizard needs someone who can explain things to actual humans.

Accountability: It's easy to slack when no one's watching. Teammates keep you honest, motivated, and showing up even when you'd rather watch Netflix and pretend your goals don't exist.

Resilience: When you're down, your party picks you up. When they're struggling, you return the favor. Together, you're exponentially harder to defeat.

Amplified Impact: Two people working in sync accomplish more than two people working separately. That's not motivational fluff—that's the mathematical reality of synergy.

Pro Tip: Think of your party like a deck in a trading card game. Each member should serve a purpose, and the combination should be greater than the sum of its parts.

I learned this lesson the hard way years ago, trying to launch a training platform entirely on my own. I had the vision, the drive, and enough caffeine to power a raid guild. What I didn't have was a designer, a developer, or anyone to tell me my brilliant idea had a fatal flaw. Six months of solo grinding later, I had nothing to show for it. The next time, I built a team first—and we shipped in half the time with twice the quality.

Step 2: Recruit Your Dream Party (Strategically)

Every RPG starts with the same question: who do you want in your party? Do you grab the high-damage rogue, the defensive tank, or the bard who keeps everyone's morale up? In life, your party members are the people you rely on for support, guidance, collaboration, and the occasional reality check.

The key is intentionality. Don't just accept whoever shows up—recruit strategically.

How to build your party:

Define the Roles You Need: Are you looking for a mentor who's been where you want to go? An accountability partner who'll call you out when you slack? A collaborator with complementary skills? A cheerleader who believes in you even when you don't? Identify the gaps and recruit accordingly.

Look for Complementary Strengths: A party full of identical builds is headed for disaster. If you're a big-picture visionary, find someone detail-oriented. If you're all execution, find someone who can strategize. If you're the tank, you need DPS and healing—period.

Prioritize Character Over Credentials: Skills can be learned. Integrity, reliability, and a genuine willingness to contribute? Those are harder to find. Choose people you trust and respect, even if their resume isn't perfect.

Test the Chemistry: Before making someone a permanent party member, try a few small quests together. Work on a minor project. Have real conversations. Chemistry matters more than most people realize. You'll be in the trenches with these people—make sure you actually like them.

Pro Tip: Not everyone you meet will make the cut. Think of it like drafting a competitive deck—you're selecting the best possible companions for your specific goals, not collecting every card in existence.

Step 3: Build Synergy Through Clear Strategy

Here's where most teams fall apart: they have good people but no cohesive strategy. You wouldn't charge into a raid boss without discussing mechanics, and you shouldn't tackle real-world challenges without a plan.

Synergy is the secret sauce that makes good teams great. In gaming, synergy happens when abilities complement each other—the healer keeping the tank alive while DPS eliminates threats. In life, synergy is about combining unique strengths to maximize effectiveness.

How to create synergy:

Understand Roles and Responsibilities: Every player has a job. Know exactly what each team member is responsible for and how their contribution fits into the bigger picture. Ambiguity breeds conflict.

Play to Strengths: Don't ask the rogue to tank or the healer to nuke. Identify what each person does best and assign tasks accordingly. This isn't about rigid roles—it's about intelligent allocation.

Develop Shared Strategy: Define the goal clearly. What does success look like? What are the major challenges you'll face? How will you handle them? Everyone needs to understand the game plan.

Communicate Constantly: Keep information flowing. Regular check-ins, updates, and honest feedback ensure everyone stays aligned. Synergy dies in silence.

Stack Your Buffs: Combine complementary skills deliberately. Pair the visionary with the executor. Match the technical expert with the communicator. Time your efforts for maximum impact.

Pro Tip: Treat team synergy like a well-tuned deck in Magic: The Gathering—each card has a purpose, and when they work together, they're unstoppable.

Step 4: Manage Dynamics and Navigate Conflict

Even the best parties hit rough patches. Maybe someone isn't pulling their weight. Maybe two members clash over strategy. Maybe that one person keeps standing in fire and refusing to acknowledge it's a problem.

Party tensions are inevitable. How you handle them determines whether your team thrives or implodes.

How to manage party dynamics:

Communicate Early and Often: Don't let small problems fester into catastrophic ones. Surface issues, expectations, and concerns before they metastasize.

Address Conflicts Directly: When tensions arise, deal with them respectfully but immediately. Ignoring a debuff just makes it worse. Have the conversation. Clear the air.

Focus on Solutions, Not Blame: Instead of pointing fingers, work together to find a path forward. "How do we fix this?" is infinitely more productive than "Whose fault is this?"

Keep the Bigger Picture Visible: Remind everyone why you're on this quest in the first place. Shared goals can put petty disagreements into perspective and reunite the party around what matters.

Adapt Roles as Needed: People change. Circumstances change. Be willing to adjust responsibilities, redistribute work, or even part ways if the current setup isn't working.

Know When to Remove Toxic Players: Some people drain more energy than they contribute. If someone consistently harms the party despite clear feedback, protecting the group means letting them go. It's not personal—it's tactical.

Pro Tip: Treat party dynamics like a raid encounter—constant awareness, quick adjustments, and don't let anyone drag the whole group into a wipe.

Step 5: Use Tools and Systems to Stay Coordinated

In gaming, managing resources and tracking objectives is critical to success. The same is true for collaborative work. Without proper organization, even the best teams fall apart.

How to stay organized:

Use Task Management Tools: Apps like Trello, Asana, Notion, or even a shared Google Doc can track progress, assign tasks, and keep everyone on the same page.

Create Shared Resources: Whether it's a Google Drive folder or a Discord channel, make sure everyone has access to the information they need when they need it.

Schedule Regular Check-Ins: Weekly or biweekly meetings to discuss progress, address challenges, and adjust plans. Consistency beats intensity.

Build Feedback Loops: Regular retrospectives where you ask "What went well? What could improve?" This keeps the team learning and adapting.

Celebrate Milestones: When you hit checkpoints, acknowledge them. Recognition boosts morale and reinforces the value of teamwork.

Pro Tip: Treat your collaborative tools like your inventory system—keep them organized, accessible, and actually use them instead of letting them gather dust.

Bio Break: AFK for a Minute!

You've got the fundamentals down—recruitment, synergy, strategy, conflict management, and organizational systems. But this is the advanced guide. We're not settling for a functional team. We're building a legendary guild that tackles epic challenges, bounces back from failure, and leaves a legacy.

Next up: the advanced tactics that separate good teams from the ones people tell stories about.

Step 6: Tackle Epic Boss Battles Together

Every team faces its share of epic boss battles. In life, these might look like major deadlines, high-stakes projects, launching a business, or navigating a crisis. The key to victory lies in your team's ability to strategize, execute, and adapt under pressure.

How to slay bosses together:

Break the Fight Into Phases: Just like a multi-phase raid boss, divide massive challenges into smaller, manageable steps. Phase 1: Preparation. Phase 2: Execution. Phase 3: Refinement. This prevents overwhelm and creates clear progress markers.

Call Out Mechanics: Communicate clearly about what's happening and what each team member needs to do. "Tank needs help!" "DPS burn the adds!" "Healer out of mana!" Real-time updates keep everyone coordinated.

Use Cooldowns Wisely: Save your team's energy, resources, and focus for the moments that matter most. Don't burn out on trash mobs when the real boss is three phases deep.

Adapt When Things Go Sideways: No strategy survives contact with the boss. When the plan fails—and it will—stay calm, pivot quickly, and adjust tactics on the fly. Panic wipes more raids than mechanics.

Learn From Attempts: Every failure teaches you something about the boss's attack patterns. Debrief after each attempt, adjust strategy, and come back stronger.

Pro Tip: Treat epic challenges like raid bosses—intimidating at first, but totally conquerable with the right strategy, coordination, and refusal to quit.

Step 7: Build Resilience Through Failure

Your team is going to fail. Repeatedly. Spectacularly. Maybe the strategy was flawed. Maybe someone missed a key mechanic. Maybe you were just unlucky. The important thing isn't avoiding failure—it's how you bounce back.

How to build team resilience:

Debrief Without Blame: After setbacks, analyze what went wrong objectively. Focus on mechanics, not personal attacks. "We need better communication" beats "You screwed up" every time.

Encourage a Growth Mindset: Remind your team that failure isn't the end—it's data. Every wipe teaches you something about the encounter. Collect enough data, and you crack the code.

Support Each Other: When morale dips, lift each other up with encouragement, humor, and perspective. Sometimes the best thing you can do is acknowledge that yes, this sucks, but we're still in this together.

Celebrate the Effort: Even in failure, acknowledge the teamwork, courage, and progress your team has made. Resilience grows from recognizing that trying and failing beats never trying at all.

Pro Tip: Treat resilience like a party-wide buff—it protects everyone from burnout and keeps the team moving forward even when the odds look terrible.

Step 8: Keep Momentum and Engagement Alive

In gaming, burnout is real. The healer's tired of spamming heals. The DPS feels underappreciated. The grind starts feeling like... well, a grind. Keeping your team engaged means ensuring everyone feels valued, motivated, and excited about what you're building together.

How to maintain engagement:

Rotate Responsibilities: Give team members chances to explore new roles or challenges. Fresh experiences prevent stagnation and reveal hidden talents.

Recognize Contributions: Share credit generously. When the party wins, make sure everyone gets recognition. Public acknowledgment costs nothing and means everything.

Set New Goals Regularly: Once a quest is complete, define the next objective. Having something to work toward maintains momentum even after major victories.

Infuse Fun Into the Process: Add humor, friendly competition, or unexpected elements that keep collaboration enjoyable. The best teams work hard but genuinely like working together.

Plan the Next Adventure: Don't wait too long between quests. Having the next challenge visible on the horizon keeps energy high.

Pro Tip: Treat engagement like a daily login bonus—it doesn't have to be huge, but consistent attention keeps everyone coming back for more.

Step 9: Scale Your Impact Without Losing Your Soul

A successful guild doesn't stay small forever. As you grow, you'll face new challenges—more members to coordinate, bigger goals to pursue, increased complexity to manage. Scaling effectively means expanding impact without losing what made the team special.

How to scale smart:

Delegate Leadership: You can't do everything yourself. Identify trusted members who can take ownership of specific areas. Great teams have multiple leaders, not one exhausted bottleneck.

Systematize What Works: Document your processes, communication norms, and decision-making frameworks. This makes onboarding easier and ensures consistency as you grow.

Maintain Culture Intentionally: Culture doesn't scale automatically. Be explicit about values, model desired behaviors, and address deviations quickly. What got you here might not get you there, but your core identity should remain intact.

Create Win-Win Scenarios: As you expand, ensure that collaborations benefit everyone involved. Align individual goals with group missions so everyone has skin in the game.

Welcome New Members Thoughtfully: Growth is good, but not at the expense of chemistry. Bring in people who align with your values and will strengthen rather than dilute your culture.

Pro Tip: Scaling is like upgrading your guild hall. It takes investment and planning, but the expanded capacity opens up possibilities that weren't available at starter level.

Step 10: Leave a Legacy Worth Remembering

At the end of the day, it's not just about completing quests or slaying bosses—it's about the mark your team leaves on the world. Great guilds aren't just remembered for victories. They're remembered for how they worked together, supported each other, and inspired others to dream bigger.

How to build lasting legacy:

Document Your Journey: Capture achievements, lessons learned, favorite moments, and epic failures. These stories become the lore that inspires future players. Create your own guild history.

Mentor the Next Generation: Share what you've learned with people coming up behind you. Your knowledge multiplied across others is how your impact extends beyond your own efforts.

Build Something That Lasts: Focus on creating value that endures—relationships, systems, contributions to communities that will continue producing benefits long after you've moved on to new adventures.

Stay Connected: Even as members move to different quests, maintain the bonds you've built. The best guilds become lifelong networks, not temporary alliances of convenience.

Celebrate the Relationships: At the end of the campaign, the most valuable loot isn't achievements or rewards—it's the people you fought alongside. Those relationships are what make the whole journey worth it.

Pro Tip: Legacy is the ultimate achievement badge. It's earned through consistent contribution and genuine care for something bigger than yourself.

Your Party Is Your Power-Up

Life is hard enough without trying to solo it. By building a strong party, creating genuine synergy, and committing to something bigger than individual success, you're not just improving your odds—you're creating a journey that's richer, more resilient, and infinitely more rewarding.

The best teams I've ever worked with weren't the ones with the most talent or the biggest budgets. They were the ones where everyone showed up for each other, communicated honestly, adapted quickly, and refused to quit when things got hard. They understood that the party itself—the relationships, the trust, the shared purpose—was the real achievement.

Solo runs make for good war stories. But the victories that actually matter? Those happen when your guild shows up, coordinates perfectly, and crushes challenges that would have been impossible alone.

In the next chapter, we'll explore how feedback systems turn good teams into legendary ones. Because even the strongest party can always level up—and feedback is the mechanic that makes continuous improvement possible.

Until then, keep recruiting strategically, keep building synergy, and keep proving that multiplayer mode isn't just the best way to play—it's the only way to build something that lasts.

Now go find your party. The best loot is waiting.

Chapter 8: The Feedback Loop - Your Life's HUD

Every game has a HUD—that constant stream of data floating at the edge of your screen, telling you exactly what's working and what's about to get you killed. Health bar dropping? Better find cover. Ammo running low? Stop spamming shots. Minimap showing enemies flanking from the left? Time to adjust your strategy.

Now imagine playing without it. No health bar. No ammo count. No radar. Just you, stumbling blindly through a raid boss fight, hoping you're not about to walk into a one-shot mechanic. Sounds like a nightmare, right?

That's exactly what life feels like when you're operating without feedback.

I learned this the hard way during a team project early in my career. We worked for months on what we thought was a brilliant initiative, only to have it implode during the final presentation. Turns out, there were problems everyone could see—everyone except us. No one had spoken up. No one had shared the concerns. We'd been running headlong into a wipe, and our HUD had been switched off the entire time.

Here's the thing most people don't realize: **feedback isn't just useful. It's the entire game's operating system.** Without it, you're essentially running a speedrun blindfolded—sure, you might finish, but the results will probably be ugly, and you'll waste months grinding in the wrong direction.

This chapter is about turning feedback into your superpower—both the feedback you get from others and the internal HUD you develop yourself. Because the best players don't wait for someone else to tell them their aim is off. They know it the moment the combo breaks.

Part I: Understanding Feedback as a Game Mechanic

Let's break this down, gamer-style. Feedback is essentially your in-game tutorial system—it tells you what's working, what isn't, and how to optimize your approach. It's the glowing red weak spot on a boss. The "You're Going the Wrong Way" alert. The post-match stats that reveal your accuracy was a pathetic 22%.

It stings, sure. But it's also your most powerful tool for improvement.

Why feedback is non-negotiable:

1. It Reveals Blind Spots
Everyone has weaknesses they can't see from their own camera angle. Maybe you interrupt people without realizing it. Maybe your reports are confusing. Maybe that "funny" comment in meetings actually makes people uncomfortable. Feedback from others reveals what you can't observe from first-person view.

2. It Validates What's Working
Good feedback isn't just about fixing problems—it's about recognizing strengths. When someone tells you that your presentation crushed it, you know to keep doing whatever you did. That's data worth having.

3. It Prevents Stagnation
Without feedback, you'll keep using the same outdated strategies, wondering why they're not working anymore. Feedback keeps you adapting to the current meta instead of playing last season's patch.

4. It Builds Trust
Teams that give honest feedback are teams that trust each other. They're saying, "I care enough about our success to tell you the truth." That's worth more than a hundred empty compliments.

Pro Tip: Think of feedback like your party's voice chat. Without it, everyone's just guessing what everyone else is doing. With it, you're coordinating, adapting, and winning.

Part II: Mastering the Art of Receiving Feedback

Let's be honest—getting feedback can feel like taking a critical hit in PvP. Your first instinct is to get defensive, explain yourself, or mentally compose a list of reasons why the other person is wrong.

Resist that urge.

The best players aren't the ones who never get criticized; they're the ones who use criticism to level up. Every piece of feedback is data. Some of it will be useful. Some of it won't. Your job is to extract the value without letting your ego turn it into a boss fight.

How to Receive Feedback Like a Champion:

1. Listen First, React Second
Before you respond, make sure you actually understand what's being said. Ask clarifying questions if needed. Half the time, people getting defensive are arguing against something that wasn't even said.

2. Assume Good Intent
Most people giving you feedback aren't trying to hurt you. They're trying to help you—or help the team. Start from that assumption. The few who *are* being malicious? Their feedback loses power when you refuse to take it personally.

3. Separate the Message from the Delivery
Sometimes feedback comes wrapped in frustration or poor phrasing. That doesn't make it invalid. Look past the packaging to find the actual point. If someone says "You're always late," translate that to "My time feels disrespected when meetings start behind schedule."

4. Don't Take It Personally
Remember, feedback is about your actions, not your worth as a person. "That presentation was unclear" isn't "You're stupid." "The deadline was missed" isn't "You're a failure." Separate yourself from the critique.

5. Look for the Truth
Even the harshest feedback usually contains a kernel of truth. Find it. Use it to level up. Everything else is just packaging.

6. Say Thank You
Yes, even if the feedback feels like a debuff. Gratitude shows maturity and keeps the lines of communication open for future input—which you absolutely want, even when it's uncomfortable.

7. Decide What to Do With It
Not all feedback is valid. Not all valid feedback is worth acting on immediately. Sit with it, evaluate it honestly, and then decide whether to implement it. But make that a conscious choice, not a defensive reflex.

Pro Tip: Treat feedback like XP from a tough quest. It might not feel great in the moment, but it's exactly what you need to level up.

Part III: Giving Feedback That Actually Helps

Giving feedback is like casting a support spell. Done right, it buffs your teammate and sets them up for success. Done wrong, it's a critical hit to their confidence that leaves everyone worse off.

The problem? Most people are terrible at giving feedback. They're either too vague ("You need to do better"), too harsh ("That was a disaster"), or so wrapped in compliments that the actual message gets lost ("Great job! I mean, the client hated it, but great effort!").

How to Give Feedback That Lands:

1. Be Specific
"Your presentation was unclear" isn't actionable. "The third slide had too much data—I counted eight charts—and it lost the audience" gives them something concrete to fix.

2. Focus on Behavior, Not Personality
Say "The deadline was missed" instead of "You're unreliable." One addresses an action that can change; the other attacks a person's character. People can change behaviors. They can't change past you deciding they're fundamentally flawed.

3. Offer a Path Forward
Feedback without solutions is just criticism. Include what they could do differently next time. "Instead of eight charts, maybe

highlight the three that directly support your main point, and include the rest in an appendix."

4. Choose Your Moment
Timing matters. Giving feedback right after a failure, when emotions are high, rarely lands well. Wait until everyone's had a chance to cool down and actually process information rationally.

5. Balance the Message
This doesn't mean the "compliment sandwich" (everyone sees through that). But acknowledging what went right alongside what needs work makes the feedback easier to receive and act on. "Your energy was great, and you clearly know the material—the structure just needs tightening."

Pro Tip: Use the SBI method: **Situation, Behavior, Impact.** "In yesterday's meeting [situation], when you interrupted the client [behavior], it made us look unprepared [impact]." Clean, clear, actionable.

Part IV: Building Feedback Systems (Team and Personal)

One-off feedback is fine, but the real power comes from systems—consistent, repeatable loops that ensure information keeps flowing. The best guilds don't just talk after a wipe; they have regular strategy sessions, performance checks, and after-action reviews.

For Teams: Creating a Feedback-Friendly Culture

1. Lead by Example
If you're the one asking for feedback first, others will follow. Say things like, "What could I have done better in that meeting?" and actually listen to the answers. When leaders model vulnerability, it signals that honest feedback is valued, not punished.

2. Make It Regular
Don't save feedback for annual reviews or post-disaster autopsies. Build it into weekly check-ins, project debriefs, or even casual conversations. The more routine it becomes, the less scary it feels.

3. Separate Feedback from Judgment
Feedback is about actions, not worth. When your team

understands that critique isn't personal—it's practical—they'll be more willing to engage with it.

4. Schedule Regular Retrospectives
Whether it's weekly, biweekly, or after major projects, create dedicated time for "What went well? What could improve?" Make it blameless. Make it constructive. Make it routine.

5. Use Anonymous Channels When Appropriate
Sometimes people need the safety of anonymity to share hard truths. Anonymous feedback surveys can surface issues that would never come up face-to-face. Just make sure you act on what you learn—nothing kills feedback culture faster than asking for input and then ignoring it.

For Yourself: Developing Your Internal HUD

Here's the hard truth: you won't always have a party member standing by to tell you your aim is off. In the single-player campaign of life, you are often the player, the coach, and the commentator all at once.

If you rely solely on other people for feedback, you're playing with lag.

1. Conduct Weekly Self-Audits
In competitive gaming, pro players watch their own replays. They don't just celebrate the headshots; they scrutinize the misses. You need to do the same.

Once a week, review your "gameplay":

- **Check your combat logs:** Look at your calendar and bank account. They don't lie. You might *feel* like you worked hard, but if the logs show 15 hours of scrolling and zero progress on your Main Quest, that's the data you need to accept.

- **Review your cooldowns:** Did you burn out by Wednesday? That's feedback that your stamina management is poor. Did you procrastinate until the deadline? That's feedback that your initiation mechanics need work.

- **Rate your performance:** Give yourself a literal score for the week. S-Rank? Barely scraped by with a C? Be honest—nobody else is looking at this scoreboard.

2. Master the Post-Mortem
When you fail a quest—miss a deadline, break a diet, lose a client—stop and ask: *What actually caused the wipe?* Was it lack of skill (you didn't know how), lack of gear (you didn't have the tools), or just bad RNG (random bad luck)?

Use the "**Five Whys" cheat code:** Ask "Why?" five times to get to the root cause.

- *I missed the gym.* Why? *I was too tired.* Why? *I stayed up too late.* Why? *I was doom-scrolling.*
- **The Fix:** The problem isn't the gym; the problem is your phone usage at night. You just found the root glitch.

No self-flagellation. This isn't about beating yourself up. It's about debugging.

3. Listen to the Game
Your life is constantly giving you haptic feedback, but most of us have the controller vibration turned off.

We ignore the headache (stamina warning). We ignore the bouncing checks (resource warning). We ignore the lack of enthusiasm (morale warning).

How to interpret the game signals:

- **Resistance is data:** If a task feels excruciatingly hard every single time, the game is telling you something. Maybe you're under-leveled for this quest, or maybe you're using the wrong class abilities. Don't just push harder; look at the mechanics.
- **Silence is feedback:** If you send 50 resumes and get zero responses, the game is giving you loud feedback. Your "attack" isn't landing. Stop spamming the same button. Change your resume and try a different strategy.

- **Results are neutral:** If the scale hasn't moved, or the savings account hasn't grown, that isn't the universe punishing you. It's the physics engine telling you that your input doesn't equal the desired output yet.

4. Apply Hotfixes (Immediate Corrections)
The best players adjust in real-time. This is the **Hotfix**—a small, immediate adjustment you make mid-gameplay to keep the run alive.

- The moment you realize you've been scrolling social media for 20 minutes, don't spiral into guilt. Just apply a hotfix: stand up, drink water, reset.
- If you walk into a meeting and realize your "Aggressive" stance is failing, don't commit to the wipe. Hotfix your tone to "Diplomatic" immediately.
- You don't need to rebuild your entire character sheet every time something goes wrong. Sometimes you just need to adjust your sensitivity settings.

Pro Tip: The faster the feedback loop, the faster the learning. Don't wait for the Game Over screen to heal.

Part V: Advanced Feedback Tactics

Now let's level up with advanced strategies for handling the tricky stuff: difficult conversations, feedback bias, and making feedback stick even when resistance is high.

Navigate Difficult Feedback Conversations

Not all feedback is easy. Sometimes you have to tell someone they're not meeting expectations. Sometimes you have to address behavior that's affecting the whole team. These conversations are uncomfortable, but avoiding them only makes things worse—like ignoring a boss mechanic and hoping it goes away.

How to handle tough feedback:

1. Prepare Ahead of Time
Know exactly what you need to say and what outcome you're

looking for. Winging it leads to rambling, confusion, or saying something you'll regret.

2. Be Direct but Respectful
Sugarcoating serious issues does no one any favors. State the problem clearly, but without attacking the person's character. "I've noticed the last three deadlines were missed, and it's affecting the team's ability to deliver" is clear and factual.

3. Give Them Space to Respond
After delivering the feedback, stop talking. Let them process and react. You'll learn a lot from how they respond.

4. Focus on Solutions
Difficult feedback should still point toward improvement. What needs to change? How can you support that change? What does success look like?

5. Follow Up
One conversation rarely fixes everything. Check in afterward to see how things are progressing and offer continued support.

Pro Tip: Treat difficult conversations like boss fights—prep your strategy, stay calm under pressure, and don't panic when things get intense.

Recognize and Counter Feedback Bias

Here's an uncomfortable truth: feedback isn't always fair. It's filtered through the biases of whoever's giving it. Studies show that women and minorities often receive vaguer, less actionable feedback than their counterparts. High performers sometimes get a pass on bad behavior, while others get scrutinized for minor mistakes.

Great teams and individuals are aware of these biases and actively work against them.

How to counter feedback bias:

1. Standardize Your Criteria
Use clear, consistent rubrics for evaluation. When everyone's measured against the same standards, bias has less room to creep in.

2. Gather Multiple Perspectives
Don't rely on one person's feedback. Get input from several sources to create a fuller, fairer picture.

3. Check Yourself
Before giving feedback, ask: Would I say this to everyone, or just this person? Am I focusing on outcomes, or am I being influenced by assumptions?

4. Create Accountability
Make feedback discussions transparent where appropriate. When people know their input might be reviewed, they tend to be more thoughtful.

Pro Tip: Bias is like lag—you don't always notice it, but it messes with your accuracy. Build systems that compensate for it.

Handle Resistance to Feedback

Not everyone welcomes feedback with open arms. Some people get defensive. Others dismiss it entirely. A few will nod along and then change absolutely nothing. Resistance is normal—but it doesn't have to derail your feedback culture.

How to work through resistance:

1. Understand the Root Cause
Is the resistance about the feedback itself, or something deeper? Fear of failure, past negative experiences or lack of trust can all create barriers.

2. Stay Patient
Changing how someone receives feedback doesn't happen overnight. Consistent, fair, supportive feedback over time can gradually lower defenses.

3. Make It Collaborative
Instead of delivering feedback as a verdict, frame it as a joint problem-solving exercise. "Let's figure this out together" feels different than "Here's what you did wrong."

4. Know When to Escalate
If resistance is persistent and affecting performance or team dynamics, it may need to become a formal performance conversation rather than a coaching conversation.

Make Feedback Your Superpower

When feedback flows freely—when it's given well, received well, and acted upon—something remarkable happens. You stop repeating the same mistakes. Communication improves. Trust deepens. Performance climbs.

For teams, feedback becomes your competitive advantage. For individuals, it becomes your reality check—the thing that keeps you grounded in actual data instead of comfortable delusions.

The best teams I've ever worked with weren't the ones with the most talent or the biggest budgets. They were the ones where feedback was oxygen—constant, essential, and completely natural. They could course-correct in real time. They spotted problems before they became disasters. They turned every project, successful or not, into fuel for the next one.

And the most successful individuals I know? They're the ones who developed an internal HUD so accurate that they can debug their own errors before anyone else even notices the glitch.

That's the power of feedback done right.

It transforms a group of individuals into a genuine team—one that learns faster, adapts quicker, and achieves things that none of them could accomplish alone.

And it transforms you from someone who's just grinding blindly to someone who's optimizing every action, learning from every failure, and constantly leveling up.

Without feedback, you're flying blind—making the same mistakes, missing opportunities to improve, and hoping effort alone will be enough.

With it, you've got a constant stream of information that keeps you aligned, adapting, and leveling up.

Stop arguing with the game mechanics. If you jump off a cliff and take fall damage, don't blame gravity. Pack a parachute next time.

Trust your internal HUD. Be your own dev team. And remember: **the ultimate feedback isn't a trophy or a paycheck. It's the quiet confidence of knowing you played the level exactly the way it was meant to be played.**

CHAPTER QUEST: Build Your Feedback System

Time to stop reading and start implementing. Here's your quest for this chapter:

Main Quest: The 30-Day Feedback Challenge

For the next 30 days, commit to the following:

Week 1: Seek Feedback

- Ask three different people for specific feedback on your work, communication, or a project
- Use this exact phrase: "What's one thing I could do differently to be more effective?"
- Write down what you hear without defending or explaining

Week 2: Give Feedback

- Give three pieces of constructive feedback using the SBI method (Situation, Behavior, Impact)
- Balance critique with recognition of what's working
- Follow up within 48 hours to see how it landed

Week 3: Self-Audit

- Conduct your first weekly self-audit
- Review your calendar, bank account, and major tasks

- Rate your week's performance (S, A, B, C, D, F)
- Identify one "root glitch" using the Five Whys method

Week 4: Build the System

- Schedule recurring feedback sessions (weekly team check-ins or monthly one-on-ones)
- Create your personal self-audit template
- Apply at least three hotfixes in real-time during the week

Micro-Quests (Complete Any Three):

⚔☐ **The Gratitude Quest:** Thank someone who gave you hard feedback in the past that helped you grow

⚔☐ **The Mirror Quest:** Record yourself in a meeting or presentation, then watch it and note three things to improve

⚔☐ **The Anonymous Quest:** Send an anonymous feedback survey to your team or friends (Google Forms works great)

⚔☐ **The Post-Mortem Quest:** Choose one recent failure and do a full Five Whys analysis

⚔☐ **The Bias Check:** Review the last three pieces of feedback you gave others. Would you have said the same things to everyone?

Level-Up Questions:

- What's one piece of feedback you've been avoiding giving someone? Why?
- What's one piece of feedback about yourself that you know is true but keep ignoring?
- If your life had a HUD, what metrics would you want displayed at all times?
- Who in your life gives you the most honest, useful feedback? Have you thanked them recently?

Next Level Preview:

You've got your feedback loops running. You know how to give it, receive it, and use it to optimize your game. In the next chapter, we're taking it to the next level: **Overcoming Obstacles and Boss Battles.** Because knowing what needs to improve is one thing. Actually defeating the big challenges standing between you and your goals? That's where the real game begins.

Keep the feedback flowing, and remember: **every critique is just another data point on your path to becoming legendary.**

Chapter 9: Leveling Up Your Skill Tree — Advanced Progress Systems

Basic XP tracking? That's tutorial stuff. You've mastered the fundamentals—setting goals, building habits, tracking progress. But if you've ever played an RPG past the first few hours, you know the early-game mechanics only get you so far. Eventually, you need talent trees, prestige systems, and advanced builds to keep climbing. Life works the same way.

This chapter is about taking your personal progression system from beginner to endgame. We're going to explore how to build a skill tree that maps your growth, implement advanced tracking systems that go beyond simple XP, and create the kind of adaptive challenges that keep you engaged when the basic grind starts feeling stale. Because here's the truth: the players who keep leveling up aren't the ones with the most raw talent—they're the ones with the best systems.

Think of this as your character's prestige mode. You've already proven you can play the game. Now it's time to optimize your build for maximum impact.

The difference between players who plateau and players who keep climbing isn't talent or luck—it's systems. It's the intentional design of how you learn, track, and adapt. By the end of this chapter, you'll have the blueprint for a progression system that doesn't just work for the next month, but for the rest of your life.

Step 1: Map Your Personal Skill Tree

Every great RPG has a skill tree—a visual representation of abilities, how they connect, and what you need to unlock next. Your life should have one too. A personal skill tree helps you see where you've been, where you're going, and how different abilities build on each other.

Here's how to create your skill tree:

1. **Identify Your Core Skills:** These are your foundational abilities—the ones you've already developed and use regularly. Maybe it's communication, technical expertise, or creative problem-solving. These form the trunk of your tree.
2. **Map the Branches:** What skills connect to your core abilities? If you're strong in communication, branches might include public speaking, negotiation, and written persuasion. Each branch represents a specialization path.
3. **Mark Your Current Level:** Be honest about where you stand. Are you a novice, intermediate, or master in each area? This assessment helps you prioritize where to invest.
4. **Identify Aspirational Skills:** These are the abilities you want to develop—the locked nodes on your tree. They might feel out of reach now, but with the right prerequisites, they become achievable.
5. **Draw the Connections:** Skills don't exist in isolation. Show how mastering one ability unlocks or enhances others. This reveals efficient leveling paths you might not have noticed.

Pro Tip: Treat your skill tree like a character build in an RPG. You can't max everything, so focus on the branches that align with your goals and playstyle.

Step 2: Choose Your Leveling Path

Once you've mapped your skill tree, you need to decide how you'll actually acquire new abilities. In games, this might mean completing quests, finding trainers, or grinding specific content. In life, the options are just as varied—and choosing the right path makes all the difference.

Here's how to select your learning approach:

1. **Formal Education:** Courses, certifications, and degrees provide structured learning with recognized credentials. Best for skills that require deep, systematic knowledge.

2. **Self-Directed Learning:** Books, online tutorials, and practice on your own. More flexible and often cheaper, but requires discipline and self-assessment.
3. **Mentorship:** Learning directly from someone who's already mastered the skill. Accelerates growth through personalized feedback and real-world wisdom.
4. **Hands-On Experience:** Sometimes the only way to learn is by doing. Projects, side hustles, and volunteering provide practical application that theory can't match.
5. **Hybrid Approaches:** Mix and match based on the skill. Technical abilities might need formal training plus practice; soft skills might develop better through experience and mentorship.

Pro Tip: Different skills require different leveling strategies. Don't force a one-size-fits-all approach—adapt your method to the ability you're building.

Step 3: Implement Adaptive Difficulty

One of the biggest reasons people lose motivation is misaligned difficulty. Too easy, and you get bored. Too hard, and you rage-quit. Great games solve this with adaptive difficulty—systems that adjust challenge based on your performance. Your life progression system should do the same.

Here's how to implement adaptive difficulty:

1. **Start Where You Are:** Set initial goals based on your current level, not where you wish you were. Early wins build momentum.
2. **Scale Progressively:** Once you're hitting targets consistently, increase the challenge. Add complexity, reduce time limits, or raise quality standards.
3. **Build in Checkpoints:** Regular assessment points let you evaluate whether the difficulty is right. Adjust up or down based on results.

4. **Use Failure as Data:** If you're failing repeatedly, the difficulty might be too high—or your approach might need adjustment. Either way, failure tells you something useful.
5. **Create Stretch Goals:** Beyond your main objectives, set ambitious targets that push your limits. Even if you don't hit them, reaching helps you grow faster.

Pro Tip: Adaptive difficulty is like dynamic level scaling in an RPG. The challenge grows with you, keeping the game engaging no matter how strong you get.

Step 4: Embrace the Grind

Skill development involves grinding. Repetition. Practice. Doing the same thing over and over until it becomes second nature. The players who level up fastest aren't necessarily the most talented—they're the ones who've learned to embrace the grind instead of resenting it.

Here's how to make grinding sustainable:

1. **Find the Fun:** Even repetitive practice can be engaging if you approach it right. Gamify it—track streaks, set records, compete with yourself.
2. **Break It Into Sessions:** Long, exhausting grinds lead to burnout. Shorter, focused sessions with breaks maintain quality and motivation.
3. **Measure Progress:** The grind feels pointless when you can't see improvement. Track metrics that show you're actually getting better, even if slowly.
4. **Celebrate Micro-Wins:** Every session where you improve slightly is a win. Acknowledge it. These small victories compound over time.
5. **Remember the Payoff:** Keep your end goal visible. Why are you grinding this skill? What does mastery unlock for you? Purpose makes repetition meaningful.

Pro Tip: Treat the grind like leveling in an MMO. It's not about rushing to max level—it's about enjoying the journey and savoring each new ability you unlock.

I learned this during my own skill-building journey. Trying to master instructional design, I hit a wall where everything felt repetitive and progress seemed invisible. What saved me was tracking every small improvement—completion times, feedback scores, iteration counts. Suddenly the grind had shape. I could see the XP accumulating, even when the day-to-day felt slow.

Step 5: Use Gamified Learning Tools

Why not practice what we preach? There's an entire ecosystem of apps and platforms designed to make skill development feel like playing a game. Used well, these tools can dramatically accelerate your progress while making the process genuinely enjoyable.

Here's how to leverage gamified learning:

1. **Language Learning:** Duolingo, Babbel, and similar apps turn vocabulary and grammar into daily quests with streaks, XP, and competitive leaderboards.
2. **Coding:** Codecademy, freeCodeCamp, and LeetCode gamify programming with achievements, progress tracking, and increasingly difficult challenges.
3. **General Knowledge:** Khan Academy, Coursera, and Brilliant use progress bars, badges, and structured paths to make learning addictive.
4. **Custom Systems:** Build your own gamification layer. Use habit trackers like Habitica that literally turn your goals into an RPG, complete with damage when you miss tasks.
5. **Social Accountability:** Join communities where progress is shared and celebrated. The social element adds competition and support that solo apps can't match.

Pro Tip: Gamified learning tools are like power-leveling guides. They optimize the experience so you gain skills faster with less friction.

Bio Break: AFK for a Minute!

You've got the foundation—skill trees, learning paths, adaptive difficulty, and the mindset to embrace the grind. Now let's level up with advanced progression systems: leaderboards, automation, emerging skills, and building the kind of adaptability that keeps you relevant no matter how the meta shifts.

Step 6: Add Competition and Leaderboards

Nothing accelerates progress like healthy competition. Whether you're racing against others or trying to beat your own records, competitive elements trigger dopamine responses that boost engagement and performance. Smart players use this to their advantage.

Here's how to add competition to your progression:

1. **Find Your Rivals:** Identify people at similar skill levels who are working toward similar goals. Friendly competition pushes everyone higher.

2. **Track Public Metrics:** Sharing your progress—on social media, in communities, or with accountability partners—creates external motivation to perform.

3. **Set Personal Records:** Compete against yourself. Track your best performances and try to beat them. This works even if you have no external competitors.

4. **Join Challenges:** Many communities run time-limited challenges—30-day skill sprints, monthly goals, annual competitions. These create urgency and focus.

5. **Celebrate Rankings:** Whether you're tracking word counts, workout sessions, or sales numbers, seeing yourself climb a leaderboard is powerfully motivating.

Pro Tip: Competition is like PvP mode. It's not for everyone all the time, but when you need an intensity boost, nothing else compares.

Studies consistently show that people who compete with peers toward shared goals are significantly more likely to achieve them. There's something primal about not wanting to fall behind—use that instinct to fuel your growth rather than fighting against it.

Step 7: Automate Your Tracking

Manual tracking works, but it's tedious—and tedium is the enemy of consistency. Modern tools can automate much of your progress monitoring, freeing you to focus on actual skill development instead of data entry.

Here's how to automate your progression system:

1. **Use Integrated Apps:** Many learning platforms automatically track time spent, lessons completed, and skills developed. Let them do the work.
2. **Connect Your Tools:** Services like Zapier can link different apps, automatically logging activities in a central dashboard.
3. **Set Automated Reminders:** Use calendar apps and notification systems to prompt practice sessions, review progress, and maintain streaks.
4. **Leverage AI Analysis:** Some platforms now use AI to analyze your patterns, predict plateaus, and suggest optimizations. Take advantage of the technology.
5. **Review Dashboards Weekly:** Automation collects the data; you still need to review it. Set a weekly appointment to assess your metrics and adjust accordingly.

Pro Tip: Automation is your in-game HUD working in the background. It tracks everything so you can focus on playing well.

Step 8: Identify and Pursue Emerging Skills

The meta is always shifting. Skills that were valuable five years ago might be obsolete today, and abilities that barely exist now could be essential tomorrow. Staying relevant means keeping your finger on the pulse of emerging skills and positioning yourself early.

Here's how to spot and develop emerging skills:

1. **Follow Industry Trends:** Read publications attend conferences, and engage with thought leaders in your field. They often signal what's coming next.
2. **Watch Technology:** New tools and platforms create new skill demands. AI, automation, blockchain—each wave brings opportunities for early adopters.
3. **Listen to Hiring Signals:** Job postings reveal what organizations value. When new skills start appearing in listings, that's your cue to start learning.
4. **Experiment Early:** You don't need to master emerging skills immediately. Early experimentation builds familiarity that becomes an advantage later.
5. **Build Adjacent Capabilities:** Skills rarely emerge in isolation. If you're strong in related areas, you can pivot more easily when new abilities become important.

Pro Tip: Emerging skills are like rare crafting recipes. They might not seem essential now, but players who acquire them early gain significant advantages later.

Step 9: Cultivate Adaptability

In gaming, adaptability separates good players from great ones. When the patch notes drop and your favorite build gets nerfed, can you pivot? When a new expansion changes the meta, can you learn the new mechanics? Life demands the same flexibility.

Here's how to build adaptability:

1. **Embrace Change as Growth:** Resist the urge to cling to what you know. Every change is an opportunity to develop new capabilities.

2. **Practice Learning New Things:** The more often you learn something new, the better you get at learning itself. Make novelty a habit.

3. **Build Transferable Skills:** Focus on abilities that apply across contexts—communication, problem-solving, critical thinking. These remain valuable no matter how circumstances change.

4. **Develop a Growth Mindset:** Believe that your abilities can improve through effort. This mindset makes you more willing to tackle challenges and persist through difficulty.

5. **Stay Curious:** Curiosity drives exploration. When you're genuinely interested in how things work, adaptation becomes natural rather than forced.

Pro Tip: Adaptability is like a dynamic stat in games—it gets stronger every time you face and overcome a new challenge. Exercise it regularly.

Step 10: Build Systems for Lifelong Leveling

The endgame isn't reaching max level—it's building systems that keep you growing indefinitely. Skills decay without maintenance. Industries evolve. The players who thrive long-term are those who've made continuous development part of their identity.

Here's how to create systems for lifelong progression:

1. **Schedule Learning Time:** Block regular time for skill development. Treat it like any other non-negotiable commitment.

2. **Rotate Focus Areas:** You can't actively develop every skill simultaneously. Create cycles that give different abilities attention over time.

3. **Build Review Rituals:** Periodically reassess your skill tree. What needs leveling? What's becoming obsolete? What new branches should you add?

4. **Stay Connected to Communities:** Learning communities keep you engaged and informed. They provide accountability, resources, and motivation.

5. **Link Development to Identity:** Don't just develop skills—become someone who develops skills. When growth is part of who you are, it sustains itself.

Pro Tip: Lifelong leveling is like playing a game with infinite expansions. There's always new content, new challenges, and new abilities to unlock. The adventure never ends.

Your Skill Tree is Your Competitive Advantage

The players who dominate aren't necessarily the most naturally talented. They're the ones who've built superior systems—who track their progress obsessively, adapt their learning to their goals, and never stop adding new abilities to their arsenal. Your skill tree isn't just a planning tool; it's your roadmap to becoming the kind of player who wins consistently.

Think about where you were a year ago. Now imagine where you could be a year from now if you implemented even half of what we've covered in this chapter. The compound effect of systematic skill development is staggering. Small improvements, tracked and built upon over time, create transformations that feel almost magical in retrospect.

In the next chapter, we'll explore team mechanics—how to build synergy with your party and tackle challenges that require coordinated effort. Because individual skills matter, but the biggest achievements happen when capable players work together. Until then, keep mapping your tree, keep grinding your abilities, and keep proving that you're committed to becoming the best version of your character.

Chapter 10: Save Points and Backup Files - Recovery Systems

Every gamer knows the sinking feeling: you've been grinding for hours, making incredible progress, clearing dungeons, collecting rare loot—and then you hit a trap you didn't see coming. Game over. And because you forgot to save, you're back at the checkpoint from two hours ago, watching all that progress evaporate.

The rage quit is real.

Here's what separates experienced players from rookies: veterans obsessively create save points. They don't just save after big victories—they save constantly, creating multiple backup files, building in redundancy so that when (not if) something goes wrong, they don't lose everything.

Life doesn't have an auto-save feature. And unlike games, you can't just reload from your last save point with all your progress intact. But you can—and absolutely should—build recovery systems into your life before disaster strikes. Because disaster will strike. The boss will eventually land a critical hit. The quest will go sideways. The perfectly laid plan will encounter the real world and immediately fall apart.

Most people build their lives like a roguelike on permadeath mode—one catastrophic failure and it's game over. No safety net. No backup plan. No recovery protocol. Just hoping nothing goes seriously wrong, which is about as strategic as hoping the final boss doesn't have a second phase.

This chapter is about building save points, backup files, and recovery systems into your life before you need them. We're going to cover how to prevent catastrophic failures through redundancy, create respawn points for when you inevitably go down, and build resilience so deep that setbacks become minor inconveniences instead of life-ending disasters.

Because the goal isn't to never fail. The goal is to build a system so robust that you can fail, recover, and keep playing.

Step 1: Understand the Types of Save Points

In gaming, different save systems serve different purposes. Quick saves for minor progress. Manual saves before risky decisions. Auto-saves as a safety net. Checkpoint systems that preserve major milestones.

Life needs all of these.

Financial Save Points (The Emergency Fund): Your buffer against economic damage. This is the difference between a car breakdown being an annoying Tuesday versus a financial catastrophe. Industry standard: 3-6 months of expenses, but even $1,000 dramatically reduces life's difficulty level.

Social Save Points (Your Support Network): The people you can call when things fall apart. Not just for emotional support—for practical help. Can you call someone at 2 AM if you need a ride to the hospital? Do you have friends who'd help you move on short notice? These are save points.

Career Save Points (Plan B and C): Skills that transfer. Side income streams. Professional relationships. Updated resume. These aren't "giving up on your dreams"—they're making sure one setback doesn't end your entire game.

Health Save Points (Baseline Resilience): Basic fitness that gives you stamina reserves. Sleep habits that prevent catastrophic burnout. Mental health practices that keep you stable during chaos. This is your HP pool—keep it high.

Knowledge Save Points (Documented Systems): Your processes written down. Passwords in a manager. Important info not just in your head. When crisis hits and your brain goes offline, documentation saves you.

Pro Tip: Save points aren't pessimism—they're intelligence. The best players aren't the ones who never fail. They're the ones who can fail and keep playing.

Step 2: Build Your Financial Firewall

Let's start with the most concrete save point: money. Financial emergencies are the number one source of catastrophic life failures. Medical bills. Job loss. Car repairs. Urgent travel. Without a buffer, these force terrible decisions under pressure.

How to build financial save points:

The Starter Save (Level 1): Get to $1,000 as fast as possible. Sell stuff. Cut expenses aggressively for two months. This single save point prevents most small emergencies from becoming debt spirals.

The Job Loss Save (Level 2): Build to one month of expenses. This gives you breathing room if income disappears. You're not safe yet, but you're not immediately desperate.

The Real Buffer (Level 3): Three to six months of expenses. This is where financial stability actually begins. Job loss, medical issues, family emergencies—you can handle them without panic.

The Multiple Income Streams Save: Don't depend on a single source of income if you can avoid it. Side projects, freelance skills, passive income—these are backup files for your financial system.

The Automatic Save Feature: Set up automatic transfers the day after payday. You can't forget to save if the system does it for you. Even $50 per paycheck builds over time.

Pro Tip: Your emergency fund should be boring. High-yield savings account. Accessible but not too accessible. This isn't investment money—it's insurance against catastrophe.

I learned this one the hard way in my twenties. No emergency fund, living paycheck to paycheck, feeling invincible. Then my transmission died. $3,000 repair. I had $400 to my name. The next three months were a financial nightmare involving credit card debt, skipped meals, and stress that nearly broke me. One save point—one emergency fund—would have made that an annoying week instead of a quarter-year disaster.

Step 3: Create Your Support Network Before Crisis Hits

Money is crucial, but social support might be even more important. Humans aren't meant to solo this game. When life goes sideways—and it will—you need people who'll show up.

How to build social save points:

The Inner Circle (3-5 People): These are ride-or-die relationships. The people who'd drop everything in a real emergency. You can't have fifty of these—the relationships are too intensive. But you need at least two or three.

The Guild (10-20 People): Your broader community. Professional network. Friend group. People you see regularly who'd help if asked. Not emergency contacts, but solid relationships.

The Specialists: Therapist. Doctor. Financial advisor. Mentor. These are professional save points—people with expertise you lack who can help navigate specific challenges

The Reciprocity System: Support networks require maintenance. Show up for others. Offer help proactively Build social capital before you need to withdraw it. This isn't transactional—it's foundational.

The Regular Check-Ins: Don't only reach out during crisis. Maintain relationships consistently. The best support networks are built through regular low-stakes interaction, not just emergency calls.

Pro Tip: A support network isn't something you build when you need it—it's something you build so it's there when you need it. Plant trees before you need shade.

Step 4: Develop Career Redundancy

Relying on a single employer, single client, or single income source is playing without save points. Economic shifts happen. Companies downsize. Industries change. Clients leave You need backup plans.

How to build career save points:

Transferable Skills: Develop abilities that work across industries. Communication. Project management. Technical skills. If your specific job disappears, you can pivot rather than starting over.

Side Projects: Not to get rich—to have options. Freelance work. Consulting. Side business. These prove you can generate income independently and provide alternatives if your main gig implodes.

Professional Network: Maintain relationships in your industry. Stay visible. Contribute to communities. When you need opportunities, your network is your fastest path to them.

Updated Materials: Keep your resume current. Maintain a portfolio. Document your achievements as they happen. When you suddenly need to job hunt, you're ready to move immediately.

Skill Expansion: Regularly learn adjacent skills. If you're a developer, understand design. If you're in marketing, understand analytics. Cross-training creates internal redundancy.

Pro Tip: Career save points aren't about job-hopping—they're about never being trapped. Options are power.

Step 5: Build Health Reserves That Buffer Stress

Your physical and mental health are the foundation everything else builds on. When health fails catastrophically, everything else struggles. You need reserves.

How to build health save points:

Basic Fitness: You don't need to be an athlete, but baseline fitness is your buffer. Regular movement, basic strength, cardiovascular health—these give you stamina reserves when life gets demanding.

Sleep Systems: Consistent sleep schedule. Good sleep hygiene. Backup plans for when sleep is disrupted. Sleep debt accumulates and eventually crashes your whole system.

Mental Health Practices: Therapy isn't just for crisis—it's preventive maintenance. Meditation, journaling, stress management techniques. Build these habits when you're stable so they're automatic during chaos.

Stress Management Toolkit: Multiple ways to decompress. Exercise. Creative outlets. Social connection. When one doesn't work, you have alternatives.

Medical Baseline: Regular checkups. Dental care. Vision care. Preventive maintenance prevents emergencies. Small problems caught early don't become catastrophic failures.

Pro Tip: Health reserves are the ultimate save point. Every other system depends on you being functional enough to execute it.

Bio Break: AFK for a Minute!

You've got the core save points covered—financial buffers, support networks, career redundancy, and health reserves. These are your preventive systems, the checkpoints you create before disaster strikes.

Now let's get into advanced recovery systems: what to do when you actually hit a catastrophe, how to rebuild after major setbacks, and how to build anti-fragile systems that get stronger from stress instead of breaking under it.

This is where we separate players who survive tough levels from players who master them.

Step 6: Create Documented Recovery Protocols

When crisis hits, your brain doesn't work well. Stress, panic, and overwhelm shut down higher reasoning. You need pre-written recovery protocols you can follow on autopilot.

How to build recovery protocols:

The Emergency Contact Sheet: Names, numbers, critical info all in one place. Medical emergency? Here's who to call and in what order. Financial crisis? Here's your advisor's number and account details. Digital and physical copies.

The Crisis Decision Tree: Pre-made decisions for common emergencies. Job loss protocol: File unemployment, contact network, update resume, reduce expenses to minimum. Medical emergency: Which hospital, insurance info, who to notify. You're not making these up under stress.

The Minimum Viable Day: What's the absolute baseline to maintain during crisis? Probably: eat something, drink water, sleep, take medications if any. When everything else fails, execute the minimum viable day.

The Reset Protocol: Specific steps to get back on track after derailing. Missed a week of workouts? One 15-minute session gets you back. Haven't written in a month? One page today. The protocol is always "smallest possible action that restarts momentum."

The Information Repository: Password manager with all accounts. Important documents in one location. Medical history. Financial accounts. When you're overwhelmed, you can find what you need.

Pro Tip: Recovery protocols are like muscle memory—build them when you're calm so they're automatic during chaos.

Step 7: Understand the Respawn Mechanics

Here's the truth about catastrophic failures: you will respawn. The question is where and how fast.

In gaming, respawn points determine how much progress you lose when you die. Spawn at the checkpoint right before the boss? You're back in the fight quickly. Spawn at the beginning of the level? Massive setback.

Life works similarly. When you hit a major failure—job loss, business collapse, relationship ending, health crisis—how fast you recover depends entirely on how many save points you built before the failure.

The Respawn Hierarchy:

Level 1 Respawn (No Save Points): Complete restart. No financial buffer, no support network, no backup plans. You're starting from scratch, probably in crisis mode, making desperate decisions under pressure. This is the hardest recovery path.

Level 2 Respawn (Some Save Points): You've got some buffer. Emergency fund covers a month or two. Some people to call. Basic plan B. Recovery is still hard but not catastrophic. You have time to make decent decisions.

Level 3 Respawn (Good Save Points): Solid financial buffer. Strong support network. Multiple options. Health reserves. Recovery is manageable. You can be strategic rather than desperate.

Level 4 Respawn (Excellent Save Points): You have redundancy everywhere. The failure is annoying but not devastating. You can actually treat it as a learning experience instead of a survival situation.

Pro Tip: The time to build respawn points is before you need them. After you're already down, your options are limited.

Step 8: Build Anti-Fragile Systems (Getting Stronger from Stress)

Save points prevent catastrophic loss. But the ultimate goal is anti-fragility—building systems that actually get stronger when stressed.

Nassim Taleb's concept: fragile things break under stress, robust things resist stress, anti-fragile things improve from stress (within limits).

How to build anti-fragility:

Multiple Small Failures: Instead of one catastrophic failure, expose yourself to many small, controlled failures. This builds resilience and reveals weaknesses before they're critical. Test your systems regularly.

Redundancy in Critical Systems: Never rely on a single point of failure. Multiple income streams. Multiple relationships. Multiple skills. If one breaks, the system continues.

Optionality Everywhere: Always have more than one option. Two job leads instead of one. Multiple service providers. Backup plans for backup plans. Options are anti-fragile—they give you upside without downside risk.

Regular System Testing: Actually use your recovery protocols occasionally. Call your emergency contacts. Live on your emergency budget for a month. Test your backup systems. This reveals holes before crisis exposes them.

Build Slack Into Systems: Overstaffed is better than understaffed. More savings than you "need." More time in schedules than required. Slack absorbs shocks without system failure.

Pro Tip: Anti-fragile systems cost more upfront but dramatically reduce long-term risk. The investment is worth it.

Step 9: Recover from Catastrophic Failures (The Respawn Protocol)

Despite all your save points, sometimes you still hit catastrophic failure. Job loss. Business collapse. Major health crisis. Relationship implosion. The question isn't if this happens—it's what you do after.

The Catastrophic Failure Recovery Protocol:

Phase 1 - Survival (Days 1-7):

- Execute minimum viable day protocol only
- Activate emergency contacts for support
- Access financial save points if needed
- Postpone all major decisions
- Focus purely on basic functioning

Phase 2 - Stabilization (Weeks 2-4):

- Assess damage honestly and completely
- Activate appropriate recovery protocols

- Lean heavily on support network
- Make minimum necessary decisions only
- Create a basic forward plan

Phase 3 - Rebuilding (Months 2-6):

- Execute recovery plan systematically
- Rebuild depleted save points gradually
- Learn from the failure (what broke and why)
- Improve systems to prevent repeat failures
- Gradually return to growth mode

Phase 4 - Reinforcement (Months 6-12):

- Strengthen weak points the failure revealed
- Build even stronger save points
- Document lessons learned
- Help others who face similar challenges
- Return to normal operation

Critical Rules:

- Don't try to recover too fast
- Don't make major decisions in crisis
- Don't skip the learning phase
- Don't isolate yourself
- Don't abandon all your save points trying to recover faster

Pro Tip: Recovery from catastrophic failure is a marathon, not a sprint. Slow, steady progress beats desperate heroics.

Step 10: Maintain Your Save Points Continuously

Save points aren't set-and-forget. They require regular maintenance. Your emergency fund needs replenishing after use. Your support network needs consistent engagement. Your skills need updating. Your health reserves need protecting.

How to maintain save points:

Quarterly System Check: Every three months, review all your save points. Is the emergency fund still adequate? Are relationships maintained? Are skills current? Are recovery protocols still relevant?

Replenish After Use: When you tap a save point—use emergency funds, lean on friends, activate plan B—prioritize rebuilding it. Don't leave gaps in your safety net.

Expand Over Time: As your life grows more complex, your save points should grow stronger. More income means bigger emergency fund. More responsibilities mean more robust support systems.

Test Regularly: Actually use your systems in low-stakes situations. Take a small risk knowing you have backup. Call your emergency contacts for non-emergencies. Practice your recovery protocols.

Update for Life Changes: New job? Update career save points. New relationship? Adjust support network. New health condition? Modify health protocols. Save points should reflect current reality.

Share the Practice: Help others build their save points. Resilience is more effective when it's communal. Strong individual save points plus strong community create nearly unbreakable systems.

Pro Tip: Maintaining save points feels like overhead when everything's fine. It's insurance—you pay the premium before you need the payout.

Your Safety Net Is Your Freedom

Here's the paradox of save points: they feel restrictive when you're building them. Emergency funds mean less spending money.

Support networks require time investment. Career redundancy means effort on things that aren't your main focus.

But save points aren't restrictions—they're freedom.

Freedom to take risks because failure won't destroy you. Freedom to walk away from bad situations because you have alternatives. Freedom to pursue ambitious goals because you've protected your downside. Freedom to recover from disasters and keep playing.

The players who accomplish the most aren't the ones who never fail. They're the ones who can fail repeatedly and keep getting back up because they built robust recovery systems.

You will hit catastrophic failures in life. Your perfect plan will encounter reality and shatter. The boss will land critical hits. The carefully constructed strategy will fall apart. This is guaranteed.

What's not guaranteed is whether you have save points.

Build your financial firewall. Develop your support network. Create career redundancy. Protect your health reserves. Document recovery protocols. Test your systems. Build anti-fragility into everything.

Not because you're pessimistic. Not because you expect failure. Because you're smart enough to know that the only difference between a temporary setback and a permanent catastrophe is how well you prepared for recovery.

The game doesn't end at the first death screen. It ends when you run out of continues. So build as many continues as you possibly can.

And when—not if—you hit that game over screen, you'll respawn at your last save point, dust yourself off, and keep playing.

Because players with save points don't quit. They reload and try again.

Chapter 11: Adapting to New Levels and Life Stages

The grind is behind you, but the map just got a lot bigger. As every gamer knows, reaching a new level doesn't mean the game gets easier—it means the mechanics get more complex. The enemies get tougher, the quests become more complex, and the stakes keep rising. Life works the same way. What worked at Level 1 won't necessarily work at Level 20, and that's okay. Adapting to new levels and life stages is all part of the journey.

In gaming, adapting often means upgrading your gear, revisiting your strategy, and learning new mechanics. In life, it means embracing change, evolving your goals, and staying flexible in the face of uncertainty. This chapter is all about navigating the transitions that come with growth and ensuring you're ready for whatever challenges and opportunities lie ahead.

Adapting to new stages in life is like progressing through the rounds of a tournament-style card game like *Hearthstone* or *Magic: The Gathering*. Each round demands different strategies depending on the deck you're up against. You can't rely on the same tactics forever—you've got to adjust, swap cards, and optimize your build as the competition evolves.

Step 1: Recognize When It's Time to Adapt

In games, it's usually obvious when it's time to change your approach. Maybe you're getting one-shot by a boss, or the quest difficulty spikes suddenly. In life, the signals can be more subtle, but they're just as important to recognize.

Here's how to spot the signs that it's time to adapt:

1. **Your Current Strategy Isn't Working:** If you're putting in effort but not seeing results, it might be time to try something new.
2. **Your Goals Have Changed:** Growth often brings new priorities. What mattered at one stage might no longer align with your vision.
3. **You Feel Stuck or Unchallenged:** If the grind feels meaningless or repetitive, it's a sign that you're ready for the next level.

Pro Tip: Treat these signals like quest markers—they're guiding you toward your next adventure.

Step 2: Reassess Your Gear and Skills

In gaming, moving to a new level often means upgrading your gear and learning new abilities. In life, it's about assessing whether your current tools, resources, and habits are still serving you—or if it's time for an upgrade.

Here's how to reassess your gear and skills:

1. **Evaluate Your Toolkit:** What skills, knowledge, and resources do you have right now? Are they enough to tackle the challenges ahead?
2. **Identify Gaps:** Look for areas where you might need to improve or acquire new tools.
3. **Upgrade Strategically:** Invest time and effort into building the capabilities that will have the biggest impact on your next level.

Pro Tip: Treat upgrades like crafting—you need the right materials (time, effort, and focus) to create something truly powerful.

Step 3: Embrace the Challenge of New Levels

Every new level comes with its own set of challenges. In gaming, this might mean harder enemies, unfamiliar mechanics, or more complex puzzles. In life, it could mean taking on new responsibilities, navigating major transitions, or stepping outside your comfort zone.

Here's how to embrace the challenge:

1. **Shift Your Mindset:** Instead of fearing the unknown, see it as an opportunity to grow and learn.
2. **Break It Down:** Approach challenges one step at a time. Focus on what you can control and tackle the rest as it comes.
3. **Learn From Experience:** Every challenge teaches you something valuable. Even if you fail, you're gaining the knowledge you'll need to succeed next time.

Pro Tip: Treat new levels like boss battles—they're tough, but they're also where the most rewarding victories happen.

Step 4: Adjust Your Strategy

Just as you wouldn't use the same tactics for every boss, you can't rely on the same life strategies at every stage. Adapting your approach ensures that you're always playing to your strengths and adjusting to the demands of the moment.

Here's how to adjust your strategy:

1. **Reevaluate Your Goals:** Are your current objectives still aligned with your long-term vision? If not, it's time to refocus.
2. **Experiment With New Approaches:** Don't be afraid to try different methods, tools, or perspectives. Flexibility is key to adaptation.
3. **Seek Input From Others:** Sometimes an outside perspective can reveal opportunities or solutions you hadn't considered.

Pro Tip: Treat strategy adjustments like respeccing your character in an RPG—it's about finding the build that works best for where you are now.

Step 5: Celebrate Progress, Not Perfection

As you adapt to new levels and life stages, it's easy to focus on what's still ahead and forget how far you've come. Celebrating progress keeps you motivated, builds confidence, and reminds you that growth is a journey, not a destination.

Here's how to celebrate progress:

1. **Reflect on Your Journey:** Take time to look back at what you've achieved and how you've grown.
2. **Acknowledge Small Wins:** Every step forward is worth celebrating, no matter how small it might seem.
3. **Share Your Success:** Celebrate with your guild, friends, or mentors. Sharing your victories makes them even sweeter.

Pro Tip: Treat progress celebrations like XP bonuses—they're not just rewards; they're fuel for the next stage of your journey.

Every Level Brings New Opportunities

Adapting to new levels and life stages isn't about starting over—it's about building on what you've already achieved and stepping into your full potential. With the right mindset, tools, and strategies, every transition becomes an opportunity to grow stronger, smarter, and more resilient.

In **Part B**, we'll dive deeper into how to handle major life transitions, embrace uncertainty, and turn every new level into a stepping stone for greatness. Because the game is always evolving, and so are you.

Bio Break: AFK for a Minute!

Step into the arena, Champion and start navigating new challenges like a pro. But as every seasoned gamer knows, the deeper you get into the game, the more complex it becomes. Life's later stages don't just throw tougher enemies at you—they introduce new mechanics, unexpected twists, and moments that test your adaptability to the max.

Part B is all about handling these transitions with finesse. We'll cover how to navigate major life changes, embrace uncertainty, and turn every new level into an opportunity for growth. Because the beauty of leveling up isn't just in reaching new heights—it's in discovering what you're truly capable of along the way.

Step 6: Embrace Life's Major Transitions

In gaming, major story beats often signal big changes—your character gets a new questline, an old ally betrays you, or the world map expands to reveal uncharted territory. In life, these transitions might look like a career change, starting a family, or entering a new stage of personal growth.

Here's how to embrace life's major transitions:

1. **Acknowledge the Change:** Pretending nothing's different doesn't help. Accept that your world has shifted and prepare to adapt.
2. **Focus on What You Can Control:** You can't dictate every outcome, but you can control how you respond to the situation.
3. **Stay Open to New Opportunities:** Transitions often come with hidden blessings. Look for ways to grow, learn, or explore new paths.

Pro Tip: Treat life transitions like an open-world expansion—they're intimidating at first, but they unlock incredible new adventures.

Step 7: Handle Uncertainty Like a Gamer

Every gamer knows the thrill—and terror—of entering a new area without a map. Life's uncertainty can feel the same way: disorienting, nerve-wracking, and full of unknowns But just like in gaming, uncertainty is also where discovery and growth happen.

Here's how to handle uncertainty:

1. **Trust Your Skills:** Even when the path isn't clear, rely on the abilities and knowledge you've built so far. They'll guide you through.
2. **Take It One Step at a Time:** Don't try to figure out everything at once. Focus on the next step, then the next, and let the journey unfold naturally.
3. **Stay Curious:** Approach uncertainty with curiosity instead of fear. Ask yourself, "What can I learn from this experience?"

Pro Tip: Treat uncertainty like fog of war in a strategy game—it feels daunting, but exploring it often reveals unexpected rewards.

Step 8: Build Resilience for Long-Term Growth

In gaming, the toughest levels demand not just skill but resilience—the ability to keep trying even when the odds are stacked against you. Life's later stages require the same grit and determination.

Here's how to build resilience:

1. **Reframe Setbacks as Learning Opportunities:** Every failure teaches you something valuable. Embrace the lessons and use them to grow stronger.
2. **Develop a Support System:** Surround yourself with allies who can offer encouragement, advice, and perspective when you need it most.
3. **Practice Self-Compassion:** Be kind to yourself during difficult times. Growth takes time, and setbacks are part of the process.

Pro Tip: Treat resilience like a shield enchantment—it doesn't stop the hits, but it helps you weather them and keep going.

Step 9: Level Up Your Perspective

At higher levels, it's easy to get caught up in the grind and forget to look at the bigger picture. But perspective is one of the most powerful tools you have. It helps you stay grounded, appreciate your progress, and keep your eyes on what truly matters.

Here's how to level up your perspective:

1. **Reflect on Your Journey:** Take time to look back at how far you've come and what you've achieved.
2. **Reconnect With Your "Why":** Remind yourself of the bigger purpose behind your actions and goals.
3. **Seek Outside Input:** Sometimes, talking to a mentor, friend, or teammate can help you see things from a fresh perspective.

Pro Tip: Treat perspective like an aerial view in a strategy game—it helps you see the battlefield clearly and make smarter decisions.

Step 10: Redefine Success at Every Level

Success isn't a fixed concept—it evolves as you do. What felt like a major victory at Level 1 might seem small at Level 20, and that's okay. Redefining success ensures that your goals remain meaningful and aligned with your growth.

Here's how to redefine success:

1. **Set Goals That Match Your Current Level:** Adjust your objectives to reflect where you are now and what you're capable of.
2. **Celebrate the Journey:** Success isn't just about reaching the destination, it's about the experiences, lessons, and connections you gain along the way.

3. **Stay Open to Change:** Your definition of success will evolve as you do. Embrace the process and allow your goals to grow with you.

Pro Tip: Treat success like a dynamic questline—it changes as the story unfolds, but the rewards are always worth the effort.

Happily Learn From Your Mistakes

Learning a new skill is like playing a game on Hard Mode when you've never even done the tutorial. You're going to fail spectacularly, probably multiple times. And that's a good thing. Every missed jump, fumbled combo, or awkward misstep is teaching you something.

In gaming, we call it 'trial and error.' In life, we call it 'growth.' Either way, the point is the same: you don't improve by avoiding failure, you improve by embracing it. Every mistake is XP in disguise, pushing you closer to mastery with every attempt."*

Every Level is a New Adventure

Adapting to new levels and life stages isn't just about surviving change—it's about thriving in it. By embracing transitions, staying resilient, and continually redefining success, you turn every new stage into an opportunity for growth and discovery.

In the next chapter, we'll explore how to continuously expand your skills and embrace the idea of lifelong learning as the ultimate endgame. Because the game of life never truly ends—it just keeps getting better. Until then, keep adapting, keep growing, and keep proving that you're the ultimate player in your own story.

Chapter 12: Continuous Learning and Innovation

Mastery is a moving target. Just when you think you know the meta, the developers drop a patch update that changes everything. You've conquered new levels, adapted to life's transitions, and proven your ability to grow in the face of every challenge. But here's the thing about mastery: it's not a finish line. In gaming and life, the most successful players are the ones who embrace continuous learning and innovation as their ultimate strategy.

In this chapter, we'll dive into the power of lifelong growth and explore how to stay on the cutting edge of your personal and professional game. Whether you're refining your current skills, exploring new horizons, or dreaming up entirely new strategies, this chapter is your guide to keeping the journey fresh, exciting, and endlessly rewarding.

Continuous learning is like managing a deck in *Dominion*. You're always refining, removing weaker cards, and adding powerful new ones to stay ahead. Every decision you make—every card you buy or discard—affects your overall strategy, just like every skill you acquire shapes your personal and professional growth.

Step 1: Commit to Lifelong Learning

In gaming, there's always a new meta to master, a hidden mechanic to discover, or a secret area to explore. In life, the same principle applies: the more you learn, the more opportunities you unlock.

Here's how to commit to lifelong learning:

1. **Adopt a Growth Mindset:** Believe that your abilities and intelligence can improve with effort and practice. Every day is a chance to learn something new.

2. **Set Learning Goals:** Whether it's reading a book a month, mastering a new skill, or completing a course, create clear objectives to guide your growth.
3. **Make Learning a Habit:** Dedicate time to learning every day, even if it's just 15 minutes. Consistency is key.

Pro Tip: Treat lifelong learning like skill mastery in an RPG—it's not about rushing to max level; it's about enjoying the process and discovering new possibilities along the way.

Step 2: Explore New Horizons

One of the best ways to keep learning is to venture outside your comfort zone. In gaming, this might mean trying a new genre, experimenting with different playstyles, or exploring areas of the map you've never visited. In life, it's about seeking out experiences that challenge you, broaden your perspective, and spark your curiosity.

Here's how to explore new horizons:

1. **Try Something Completely Different:** Pick up a hobby, skill, or subject that has nothing to do with your current expertise.
2. **Network With Diverse Groups:** Surround yourself with people from different backgrounds, industries, and perspectives. They can introduce you to ideas and opportunities you'd never encounter on your own.
3. **Travel or Step Outside Your Routine:** New environments and experiences often lead to fresh insights and inspiration.

Pro Tip: Treat exploring new horizons like unlocking a hidden questline—it's unexpected, exciting, and full of potential rewards.

Step 3: Embrace Innovation

Innovation is what keeps the game interesting. In gaming, it's the new mechanics, tools, and updates that change how you play. In life, innovation means finding creative solutions, experimenting with fresh approaches, and staying ahead of the curve.

Here's how to embrace innovation:

1. **Question the Status Quo:** Don't accept "this is how it's always been done" as a valid reason. Look for ways to improve, simplify, or reimagine the systems around you.
2. **Experiment Boldly:** Try new methods, tools, or ideas—even if they fail, you'll learn something valuable.
3. **Stay Curious:** Read, watch, and explore content that challenges your assumptions and introduces you to new concepts.

Pro Tip: Treat innovation like modding a game—you're not just playing by the rules; you're rewriting them to make the experience even better.

Step 4: Share Your Knowledge

The greatest gamers don't just master the game—they teach others how to play. Sharing your knowledge amplifies your impact, strengthens your understanding, and builds a legacy that extends far beyond your individual achievements.

Here's how to share your knowledge:

1. **Mentor Others:** Offer guidance to someone just starting out in your field or skill. Helping them grow is one of the most rewarding ways to solidify your own expertise.
2. **Create and Publish:** Write a blog, record a podcast, or create videos to share your insights with a broader audience.
3. **Collaborate and Teach:** Join forums, workshops, or events where you can share your knowledge and learn from others in return.

Pro Tip: Treat sharing knowledge like forming a guild—it's not just about what you gain; it's about building a community of mutual growth.

Step 5: Make Innovation and Learning a Team Sport

The best teams constantly learn and innovate together. Whether it's a guild in a game or a team in real life, shared growth creates stronger bonds, higher performance, and more fulfilling experiences.

Here's how to foster team learning and innovation.

1. **Create a Culture of Curiosity:** Encourage your team to ask questions, challenge assumptions, and seek out new ideas.
2. **Collaborate on Learning Goals:** Set shared objectives for growth, such as attending a conference, reading a book together, or experimenting with a new process.
3. **Celebrate Collective Wins:** Recognize and reward the team's efforts to learn and innovate together.

Pro Tip: Treat team learning like a co-op campaign—it's more fun, more engaging, and more impactful when you do it together.

Learning is Your Superpower

Committing to continuous learning and innovation isn't just about staying competitive—it's about unlocking your full potential and embracing the joy of discovery. In **Part B**, we'll dive deeper into how to apply these principles to drive personal and professional success, ensuring that you're always one step ahead of the game. Because when you make learning and innovation a way of life, you're unstoppable.

Bio Break: AFK for a Minute!

For the Completionist who wants 100%, the grind for mastery doesn't stop there. Continuous learning and innovation aren't just about collecting XP—they're about using that knowledge to stay ahead, make an impact, and create something extraordinary.

In Part B, we'll focus on applying the principles of learning and innovation to drive success in your personal and professional life. We'll explore how to turn your knowledge into actionable results, foster creativity, and build a sustainable system for growth that keeps you at the top of your game.

Step 6: Turn Knowledge Into Action

In gaming, learning a mechanic is useless unless you apply it in the heat of battle. The same goes for life. Collecting knowledge is great, but its true value lies in how you use it.

Here's how to turn knowledge into action:

1. **Set Clear Goals:** Define specific, actionable objectives that align with what you've learned. For example, if you've studied public speaking, aim to deliver a presentation or host a webinar.
2. **Experiment and Iterate:** Apply your knowledge in real-world scenarios, evaluate the results, and refine your approach as needed.
3. **Track Your Impact:** Measure how your actions influence your personal or professional growth. This helps you identify what works and where to improve.

Pro Tip: Treat knowledge like a new ability in your skill tree—it's only valuable when you use it strategically to achieve your goals.

Step 7: Foster Creativity Through Innovation

Creativity is the secret sauce of innovation. In gaming, creativity leads to unconventional strategies, unexpected solutions, and game-changing moves. In life, it's what allows you to solve problems, seize opportunities, and stand out in a crowded field.

Here's how to foster creativity:

1. **Challenge Assumptions:** Ask "why" and "why not" to uncover new possibilities.
2. **Create Space for Ideas:** Set aside time to brainstorm, daydream, or explore without pressure. Sometimes the best ideas come when you're not actively searching for them.
3. **Collaborate With Others:** Creativity often flourishes when ideas collide. Work with people who bring different perspectives and skills to the table.

Pro Tip: Treat creativity like crafting rare items—it takes time, experimentation, and the right materials to create something truly unique.

Step 8: Build a System for Continuous Growth

In gaming, progression systems keep you engaged by offering consistent rewards, new challenges, and opportunities to improve. Building a similar system in life ensures that you're always learning, growing, and staying motivated.

Here's how to build your growth system:

1. **Schedule Time for Learning:** Dedicate regular blocks of time to reading, practicing, or exploring new skills.
2. **Set Milestones and Rewards:** Break your goals into smaller steps and celebrate each milestone with a meaningful reward.
3. **Review and Adjust:** Periodically assess your progress and make adjustments to your system based on what's working and what's not.

Pro Tip: Treat your growth system like a leveling framework—it keeps you engaged and ensures steady progress over time.

Step 9: Leverage Feedback for Innovation

In gaming, feedback loops help you refine your strategy, improve your performance, and adapt to new challenges. In life, feedback is just as crucial for driving innovation and achieving success.

Here's how to leverage feedback effectively:

1. **Seek Input From Multiple Sources:** Gather insights from mentors, peers, customers, and even competitors. Different perspectives provide a more comprehensive view.
2. **Act on Constructive Criticism:** Use feedback to identify areas for improvement and implement changes that drive results.
3. **Create a Feedback Culture:** Encourage open and honest communication in your personal and professional circles to foster continuous improvement.

Pro Tip: Treat feedback like a mini-map—it shows you where you're headed and highlights areas you might be missing.

Step 10: Stay Future-Focused

In gaming, the meta is always evolving. Staying competitive means anticipating changes, adapting quickly, and embracing the unknown. In life, staying future-focused ensures that you're always prepared for what's next.

Here's how to stay ahead of the curve:

1. **Invest in Emerging Trends:** Stay curious about new technologies, industries, and ideas that could shape the future.
2. **Embrace Lifelong Curiosity:** Never stop asking questions, exploring possibilities, or seeking out new knowledge.
3. **Plan for the Long Game:** Think beyond immediate goals and consider how your actions today will impact your future self.

Pro Tip: Treat future-focused thinking like scouting the battlefield—it gives you the advantage of foresight and strategic planning.

Motivation During the Grind

Here's the trick to staying motivated during the grind: treat your skill-building like a long-term progression system in an RPG. Break the skill into 'levels,' assign XP for each milestone, and reward yourself for hitting each one. For example, if you're learning a language, earning 100 XP might mean completing a chapter of a workbook, while hitting 500 XP earns you a badge or even a night out at your favorite restaurant.

This taps into the psychology of incremental progress. By gamifying your learning journey, you turn the long, sometimes tedious process of skill-building into an engaging quest with constant dopamine hits to keep you going.

Learning is Your Endgame Strategy

Continuous learning and innovation aren't just tools for success—they're a way of life. They keep you engaged, adaptable, and ready for whatever challenges and opportunities come your way. By turning knowledge into action, fostering creativity, and staying future-focused, you ensure that your growth never stops—and your potential is limitless.

In the next chapter, we'll dive into the art of building habits that last, helping you solidify everything you've learned and create a foundation for long-term success. Until then, keep learning, keep innovating, and keep proving that you're the ultimate player in the game of life.

Conclusion: Your Life, Your Game, Your Legacy

The credits are rolling.

Not the end credits—the ones that play before the post-credits scene, before the secret ending, before the game reveals that everything you just experienced was only the beginning. You've reached the final chapter of *Gamify Your Life for Success*, and if you're expecting me to wrap this up with a neat little bow and send you on your way, you haven't been paying attention.

This isn't that kind of game. And you're not that kind of player.

You picked up this book because something wasn't working. Maybe you were stuck in a grind that felt pointless—waking up, going through the motions, wondering if this was really all there was. Maybe you were staring down a boss battle that seemed unwinnable—a goal so big, a challenge so daunting, that you couldn't even figure out where to start. Or maybe you just had this nagging feeling that you were capable of more, that somewhere out there was a strategy guide for the life you actually wanted to live.

You found it. And more importantly, you read it. You showed up, chapter after chapter, absorbing strategies for quest design and habit formation and boss battles and guild building and feedback loops and skill trees. You learned how to transform the chaos of everyday existence into something that looks a lot like the games you love—complete with progress bars, level-ups, and the occasional legendary drop.

But here's what I need you to understand before you close this book: **none of that matters if you don't play.**

— ✦ —

The Seven Principles of Life Gamification

Before you step back into the arena, let me distill everything we've covered into seven core principles. Think of these as permanent buffs—passive abilities that stay equipped no matter what challenges you face. Return to them when you're lost. Recite them when you're struggling. Let them become the operating system running beneath every decision you make.

I. You Are the Player, Not an NPC

You are not a background character in someone else's story. You are not following a script written by your circumstances, your upbringing, or other people's expectations. You are the protagonist—the one holding the controller, making the choices, shaping the narrative. This means you own your decisions. You can respec your character at any time. You can abandon questlines that no longer serve you and pick up new ones that set your soul on fire.

II. Design Your Quests With Purpose

Goals without structure are just wishes floating in the void. The magic of gamification lies in deliberate quest design—main quests that give you direction, side quests that build your capabilities, daily quests that compound into transformation. Know what you're working toward. Track your progress obsessively. Break overwhelming objectives into achievable milestones.

III. Embrace the Grind

Here's a truth that separates players who level up from players who quit: the grind isn't the obstacle standing between you and the reward. The grind *is* the reward. Every repetition builds mastery. Every difficult day builds resilience. Every small victory builds the momentum that carries you through the moments when motivation disappears.

IV. Build Your Party

Solo runs make for good stories, but the biggest achievements require coordinated effort. Your party is your inner circle—mentors who guide you, accountability partners who challenge you, supporters who believe in you when you've stopped believing in yourself. Invest in these relationships. Show up for your allies without keeping score. The lone wolf fantasy is exactly that—a fantasy.

V. Learn From Every Wipe

You're going to fail. Spectacularly. Repeatedly. You'll launch initiatives that collapse, pursue paths that dead-end, and face bosses that flatten you before you even understand what happened. This isn't a bug in the system. It's the primary mechanism for growth. Every failure contains data about what doesn't work, which means you're one step closer to discovering what does.

VI. Keep Expanding Your World

The moment you stop exploring is the moment you start dying—slowly, invisibly, but surely. Great players don't just master their current content. They seek out new challenges, new skills, new territories that push them beyond the comfortable and familiar. Stay curious. Learn things that seem irrelevant to your current questline. The unknown is where the best loot hides.

VII. Leave a Legacy

Ultimately, this isn't just about your own success. The most meaningful victories are the ones that ripple outward—the people you help, the knowledge you share, the positive change you create in the lives of others. Mentor someone coming up behind you. Contribute to communities that matter. Your legacy isn't measured in achievements unlocked. It's measured in the players you inspired.

The Scrappy Rogue

Let me tell you a story.

Picture a player—let's call them a scrappy rogue—starting the game of life with no special advantages. No legendary gear passed down from previous generations. No powerful guild waiting to recruit them. Just a wooden sword of questionable durability, a half-eaten health potion, and a stubborn refusal to accept that the odds were stacked against them.

Their first boss fight was brutal. A hulking creature called Self-Doubt, with devastating attacks that drained health and motivation in equal measure. The rogue went down. Respawned at the checkpoint. Tried again. Went down faster. For a while, it looked like the game might simply be too hard, the boss too strong, the whole endeavor a waste of time.

But something happened during those repeated failures.

The rogue started noticing patterns. They learned which attacks could be dodged and which required blocking. They discovered windows of opportunity—brief moments when the boss was vulnerable. They ground out small improvements in gear and stats. They found allies who'd faced the same fight and learned from their strategies.

And eventually—not through some cinematic montage, but through hundreds of small choices accumulated over months and years—they stood victorious. Not because they were the most talented player in the game. Not because luck intervened at a crucial moment. Not because they found a cheat code that let them skip the hard parts.

They won because they refused to stop pressing start.

Here's the spoiler: that rogue is you. Or rather, that rogue is who you become when you apply everything in this book. Because the secret to winning the game of life was never talent or luck or circumstances. It was always persistence, adaptability, and the willingness to show up and play, day after day, no matter how many times the boss knocked you down.

— ✦ —

Your Final Quest

This is the part where I'm supposed to deliver a rousing speech about seizing the day and conquering your dreams. But you've read enough inspiration. What you need now is action.

So here's your final quest—not a metaphor, but an actual assignment:

Within the next 24 hours, complete these three objectives:

Objective 1: Name Your Next Boss

What's the challenge you've been avoiding? The goal that feels too big? The conversation you've been putting off? Give it a name. Write it down. Acknowledge that it exists and that you're going to face it. Bosses lose half their power the moment you stop pretending they're not there.

Objective 2: Equip One Ability

What's one skill, resource, or relationship that would help you tackle this boss? Identify it and take one concrete step toward acquiring it today. Not tomorrow. Not next week. Today. Sign up for the course. Send the message. Buy the book. Make the appointment.

Objective 3: Land the First Hit

Take the smallest possible action that moves you toward your boss. Send the email. Open the document. Make the call. Draft the outline. Do something—anything—that proves to yourself you're in this fight. The first hit is always the hardest. But once you've landed it, you've transformed from someone who's thinking about fighting into someone who's actually fighting.

The Infinite Game

Here's the truth I hope stays with you long after you've forgotten the specific strategies in these pages: **life isn't a game you win. It's a game you play.**

There's no final boss. No end credits. No moment where you've definitively "made it" and can stop trying. The most successful people you admire? They're still playing. Still grinding. Still facing new challenges and leveling up new skills. The game doesn't end when you achieve your goals—it evolves, revealing new content you couldn't have imagined from where you started.

That might sound exhausting if you're thinking about it wrong. But here's the reframe: **you get to keep playing.** Forever. Every day is a new session. Every challenge is a new quest. Every setback is a checkpoint you'll respawn from with more knowledge than you had before.

The infinite game isn't a burden. It's a gift. It means there's always another level to reach, another skill to master, another adventure waiting just beyond the horizon. It means you're never finished becoming who you're capable of becoming.

So don't play to win. Play to keep playing. Play because the game itself—the growth, the challenge, the camaraderie, the small victories and spectacular failures—*is* the reward.

One Last Thing

I'm going to keep this short, because you've got a game to play.

Thank you for trusting me to be your guide through this particular dungeon. Writing this book was one of our own main quests, (each), and knowing it might help even one player level up makes every hour of the grind worthwhile.

Here's what I believe about you, even though we've never met: you're ready. Not ready in the sense that you have everything figured out—nobody does. Ready in the sense that you have what it takes to figure it out as you go. You've got the frameworks. You've got the strategies. You've got a completely different way of seeing the challenges you face.

The player who seeks better strategies has already proven they have what it takes to use them. That's you. That's been you this whole time.

So trust yourself. Trust the systems you're going to build. Trust that every small action compounds, every failure teaches, and every new day offers fresh opportunities to level up.

Now close this book.

Open your life.

And show the world what kind of player you really are.

— ✦ —

Design your quest.

Grind for it.

Own it.

—

The next quest is yours.

Go claim it.

GAME OVER?

No.

GAME ON.

About the Authors

(The Strange Party Behind This Quest)

Ibrahim Roble — Kenyan Writer, Technology Expert & Creative Strategist

Ibrahim Roble is a storyteller, co-author, gamer, and creative strategist who believes the best ideas happen when you mix the impossible with the practical. Whether he's co-writing books about gamifying life, crafting YA fantasy worlds where kids steal from dreams, or putting monsters in the Hundred Acre Wood, Ibrahim brings an energy that makes people say, "You can't write that!" (He can. He does.)

Ibrahim holds a Bachelor of Technology in Computer and Electronic Systems, which means he understands how systems are thought, digital or otherwise. Born in Kenya and armed with real questions about truth, power, and how gaming mechanics map onto real life, he brings an analytical mind to everything he writes. As a longtime collaborator with Ken Konet, Ibrahim has co-authored multiple projects across genres, including the Dream Heist YA series and the Monsterific middle-grade series.

His approach to writing is simple: make it real, make it fun, and never let anyone tell you the idea is too wild.

Fun fact: Ibrahim's friends no longer ask him what he's working on, because the answer is always something that will either level you up or ruin your childhood. Sometimes both.

Ken Konet, M.Ed., MBA — Instructional Designer, Author & Board Game Veteran

Ken Konet is a Corporate Instructional Designer, educational consultant, and author who writes across more genres than most people read. With two MBAs and a Master's in Education, he brings a unique blend of teaching expertise and business insight to everything he creates—which explains why his books manage to be both wildly entertaining and sneakily educational.

With over 20 years of experience weaving gamification techniques into corporate training and education, Ken has seen firsthand how gaming principles can transform not just how we learn, but how we live. He grew up on board games—the kind where friendships are forged and occasionally destroyed over a game of Risk—and came to video gaming later in life, thanks to his wife Izzy, who serves as his personal video gaming coach, co-op partner, and the person most likely to yell "Why did you aggro the whole dungeon?!"

Ken lives in Florida with Izzy, where he spends his non-writing hours riding motorcycles, hiking, camping, and explaining to his wife why he absolutely needs to start another book series.

Find Ken online at www.Humbolton.com (unless he's rage-quit the internet by the time you read this).

Isabella "Izzy" Green — Professional Handywoman, Gamer & Secret Weapon

Isabella Green is a professional handywoman who runs a successful Handywoman business serving clients across three cities in Florida, Ohio and Texas. By day, she fixes what's broken. At night, she fixes Ken's terrible gaming habits.

An avid gamer who grew up with a controller in her hands, Izzy is the reason this book exists in its current form. She's the one who taught Ken that video games aren't just button-mashing—they're strategy, timing, and knowing when to let the tank pull aggro instead of charging in like an idiot. She's also his regular co-op partner for multiplayer sessions, board game nights, and the occasional DnD campaign where she inevitably rolls better than everyone else.

Izzy's contribution to this book goes beyond moral support. Her real-world experience running a business, solving problems under pressure, and literally building things with her hands gave Ken a constant reminder that gamification isn't just theory—it's how capable people already operate. She just doesn't call it that.

Together, Ken, Ibrahim, and Izzy form a team that proves the best parties are built on complementary skills, shared ambition, and the occasional argument about who gets to be the healer.

Follow their questionable life choices at: www.humbolton.com

www.ingramcontent.com/pod-product-compliance
Lightning Source LLC
LaVergne TN
LVHW010924110826
845149LV00013B/2474